Poisonous

Tommy B. Smith

A Black Diamond book.

Cover art by Drop Dead Designs.

First Rainstorm Press Edition: August 2012

Black Diamond Edition: June 2018

ISBN: 0692121242
ISBN-13: 978-0692121245

This book is dedicated to the memory of Lynn and Linda Riebow, who gave so much, yet asked so little.

1980

LIVING POISON

Harold Chambers awoke in darkness. Only a single dim light shone from overhead, and its illumination was so scarce it revealed nothing of the room's interior, aside from Harold and the metal operating table to which he was strapped. The coldness of the table permeated his naked skin from beneath, but as uncomfortable as this was, he was unable to free himself. Though he was strapped down, a strange paralysis also seemed to grip his limbs, and even without the straps he doubted he would be able to move.

A face broke through the darkness, a white face, which appeared especially peculiar in such minimal lighting. The area around the eyes was dark and sunken, but the eyes themselves were brightly manic. The lips were red. It reminded Harold of a clown's painted face.

"Nurse?" the face spoke. It tipped its absurd visage toward Harold.

Another figure emerged from the dark, a woman dressed in a white nurse's uniform. Though her features were symmetrical, beauty was somehow absent from them. She was as plain and unmemorable in appearance as anyone Harold had ever seen, which marked her a stark contrast to Clown-Face.

The nurse handed a scalpel to Clown-Face. The pale overhead light glinted from the instrument. Clown-Face looked at it briefly, then turned back to Harold. His lips stretched into a smile. The smile was calculating and sadistic.

Fear seized Harold. Clown-Face leaned over him with the shining scalpel and began to make an incision across Harold's abdominal region. Blood dripped from the surgical trail. The pain was excruciating. Clown-Face operated with deliberate slowness in making a suitable opening in Harold, and once he was satisfied, he called again for the nurse.

The nurse brought forth something terrible. Initially, Harold was unable to identify the small, wrinkled object, but his pain and fear spiked as he recognized what it was in the nurse's hands.

The baby was too small, and the wrong color. It was gray and blotched, and far more disturbing than any natural infant should appear. It had died, and its death had been premature.

Clown-Face lowered the fetus into Harold's open body. Horror and revulsion catapulted Harold into a silent frenzy, but no scream could escape his lips. Instead, he slipped into unconsciousness.

It had been over a month ago, and since that time, Harold had persistently questioned whether or not it had been a mere dream. He had woken in his bedroom as though the incident had never happened, and everything was in its proper place.

There was one unusual detail, however. The front door was unlocked. Harold always locked the front door.

He was hesitant to tell the police about what he had experienced. They would surely just laugh at him, or recommend that he see a doctor for his delusional mental state.

Harold had unquestionably changed. The transition had been gradual at first, but became more apparent with the passing of time.

He vomited another shard of his essence into the void with every single day, but with each day's passing, he woke again to walk the languid path of motions. He suffered incessantly, and yet, deep inside, he laughed with nearly every hour of his slow deterioration from this parasitic inner stain.

He now sat in front of Dr. Henderson, the third physician he had visited since that day, and since he began to suspect the worst of his condition. Dr. Henderson looked over Harold and glanced to the paper on his clipboard.

"Mr. Chambers, your test results returned, and they're excellent. I've seldom seen a healthier man."

"I'm not a hypochondriac, doctor," Harold said. His tone was listless. "I'm telling you, there's something *inside* me. Something that doesn't belong."

"We haven't been able to detect anything," Dr. Henderson replied. "Have you been taking the medication I prescribed?"

"I've taken your medication," Harold responded, and mustered an edge to his voice. "It's done nothing." Harold suddenly sensed that Dr. Henderson wasn't taking him seriously.

"If there's nothing else, then we're through here," he muttered in the doctor's direction, after the man remained quiet for several seconds. Harold stood and walked out of Dr. Henderson's office.

During the drive home, he switched on the radio. He focused on the soft, intricate melody of the classical piece, and the miasma of his mind worked to divert his concentration from haunted thoughts of his plight.

An absence of well-being had signified its inception, but as the inconsistency within him spread throughout him, the Living Poison had gradually anchored its hold within. It was devouring Harold, and on some days, he felt an eerie emptiness spawning inside. Harold was becoming detached from the prospect of the inevitable.

Acceptance: the final stage to precede his own death.

When he arrived in the driveway, he went into his home and walked straight to the liquor cabinet. He took the bottle of vodka from its place and settled onto his sofa in front of the blank television. He opened the bottle and tossed the cap aside. Harold stared lethargically at the television for a moment, and turned up the bottle to swallow all that was left in a single pull.

The burn of the alcohol never registered. He often drank this way now, perhaps hoping he could destroy the other entity in his body, although it had yet failed to yield any results. Just as he couldn't taste the alcohol, he no longer seemed to be subject to its effects.

The desired effects were lost, Harold knew, because the entity building inside of him was as prominent as ever. Harold began to wonder, then, if the thing could grow inside an unsuitable host. What if he ruined his body before this Living Poison completed its course?

He went to the laundry room, lifted the jug of bleach, and took a deep breath before he drank. He could feel only a slight burn as it gushed down his throat and entered his digestive system, but he liked the burn, because it signified that, somewhere inside, he was still alive.

The pain that churned in his stomach was dull. He acknowledged it without concern. Harold was distanced from the complications of his own suffering. More than ever, it was clear that there were two beings inhabiting the same body: Harold Chambers and the horrible internal presence.

Another sensation overrode the abstracted pain in his stomach, a stirring of the discrepancy within him. The poison had stimulated it somehow, and in seconds, he felt himself slipping out of control. His life force ebbed, and the entity inside him became stronger.

Harold was losing himself. It was consuming him.

His only remaining option pierced the numb barrier of his mind. As the Living Poison had been implanted in him on that cold, remorseless operating table, so he would have to remove it. He sensed he had little time left to act.

He forced himself toward the kitchen. He stumbled to the kitchen counter, to the knife rack. He gripped the largest steak knife available and plunged it into his own abdomen.

He sliced into his own body. The pain was foreign to him. Blood gushed. He plunged a hand inside himself, took hold of the slippery substance, and ripped his entrails out. He flung them onto the counter.

Harold collapsed to his knees. Thick blood flowed from his body in torrents. When every sensation had passed, he pulled himself to his feet and dropped the steak knife onto the counter beside the mass of internal organs.

The individual turned and walked from the room with a brief glance back at the mess on the counter.

It had no further need of such vestiges, as they had served to sustain Harold Chambers, and Harold Chambers was dead.

COLD AS DEATH

T he bridge which spanned the river, reconstructed
following the Quake of '79, was referred to by
most as the River Bridge. The area extending
along both sides of the river, the valley region of St.
Charles, was a quiet area clustered with modest homes.
The river itself, while popular for fishing, was forbidden
for swimming due to the occasional tale of the river's
abnormal undercurrent, which had claimed more than a
few victims in years past.

During the late evening hours, high above the river,
an unmarked police vehicle hummed smoothly over the
bridge. The driver of the vehicle, Detective C. J. Corbin,
took it past the end of the River Bridge and into the
downtown area. In the passenger's seat, Detective
Brandt McCullough, bleary-eyed, raised the cup to his
lips and took a sip of coffee. He grimaced.

"Can't make a decent pot of coffee to save your life,
can you, Corbin?" he muttered. Corbin glanced over, but
said nothing. He looked back to the road.

McCullough sighed. He ran a hand over his dark,
short-cropped hair and laid back. He tried to relax
against the seat and forced down another gulp of bad
coffee. He watched the road in silence.

Corbin drove them through the streets of the west
end until they entered a run-down suburban stretch. After turning onto the road of their destination, they spotted

the whirling lights of police cruisers parked in front of the plain white house.

Aside from this, and the police tape and officers on its premises, the house matched both houses to each side of it. Until this occurrence, it resembled every other to-be crime scene—an otherwise ordinary house.

Corbin wheeled the cruiser into the gravel area on the outer edge of the splotchy lawn and parked. McCullough threw back the last of his cold coffee. They jumped out to approach the home.

Halfway across the front yard, Corbin halted, his eyes fixed on the ground in front of him. McCullough followed his gaze to the bare spot on the ground and saw the blood.

With Corbin right behind him, McCullough moved to the home's front entrance. They stalked through the house, taking in their surroundings as they moved, until they reached the kitchen. McCullough gasped.

"What in the..."

He didn't finish. He didn't need to. The sight of the blood-covered wall and counter, and the steak knife on the same counter beside the heaped entrails, said plenty. Even the initial reports of the scene had not prepared them for its reality. Corbin stopped, overcome, and propped himself against one wall. He took a few deep breaths to gather himself.

"We've got to search the rest of the house," McCullough said. Though shaken, McCullough did his best to retain composure. He recalled something an old friend had told him once, many years ago.

"Courage is not a lack of fear," John Sutterfield had said, "courage is acting in spite of it."

McCullough had laughed. "So that's why you're running off to join the circus? Where did you pick up something like that, anyway?"

Sutterfield glowered. "Mark Twain."

"You knew him in person?"

"Really funny. I'm not 'running off to join the circus,' as you put it."

Of course, Sutterfield *had* run off to join the circus, or rather, to become the founder of *Sutterfield's Circus of the Fantastic.* McCullough had taken a very different road.

McCullough's was a career which landed him, at present, in the middle of—he wasn't even sure. In all his years on the force, McCullough had never seen anything like this.

"Okay," Corbin said, standing up straight. "I'm okay."

"Ready?" McCullough asked. Corbin nodded.

The two searched the rest of the house. They came across a splash of bleach here and an empty vodka bottle there. Other than the mess in the kitchen, there appeared to be no signs of violence. While Corbin remained to assess the findings McCullough headed back outside to that barely visible trail of red, which he followed to its end, a large red splotch on the pavement. He studied this for a considerable moment, contemplating it, before moving on.

McCullough looked around at the various residences and toward the ramshackle gas station a distance up the street. Chambers, or possibly his killer—whoever's trail McCullough was following—could have gone anywhere from here.

He studied the ground and every detail of his surroundings, but found nothing else. The trail was cold as death—as cold as the eyes of the dog that lay outside of the gas station, unseen by McCullough.

While McCullough began to move house-to-house, asking questions of each local home's occupant, Milt Radner sat behind the counter of the gas station. A cheap ballpoint pen and a jar of beef jerky rested on the counter beside the day's newspaper, spread open to the sports section.

Milt, a man in his mid-thirties with shoulder-length greasy hair covered by a baseball cap, had owned this place for a few years now. Today, business was slow. When the bell jingled and McCullough walked in, Milt looked up.

"Afternoon," he said. He folded the newspaper and slid it under the counter.

"Did you see anything unusual yesterday evening?" McCullough asked him. "Or last night?"

Milt studied McCullough from his boots to his tan trench coat. "You a cop?"

McCullough ignored the question. "Have you seen anything?" he asked, his tone still personable enough, but a tad less patient than before.

"I haven't seen anything. Did something happen around here?"

"Are you acquainted with Harold Chambers?" McCullough asked him. "A man who lives a block away from here?"

"I don't know," Milt said. "Customers come in all the time. Some of them I know by name, some of them I don't. What's he look like?"

McCullough produced a picture. Milt stared at it for several seconds before shaking his head.

After a few more fruitless questions, McCullough handed him a slip of paper. "Here's my number. If you see or hear *anything,* don't hesitate to let me know." He paused. "Or if you suddenly remember anything."

He left. The bell jingled again on his way out. Milt tossed the slip of paper aside. Unsure of what to make of his little visit from the police, he picked his newspaper back up.

Half an hour later, he stood up to walk outside with the glass jar of beef jerky. He walked around to the area behind the gas station, where the neighborhood strays waited expectantly.

"Here you go!" he called. The dogs ran to him, sniffing and drooling. He tossed the jerky to them. They dove for it. Slobbering gluttony ensued. They loved this stuff.

Milt noticed one of the dogs, a Basset hound named Sunday, didn't come over for the jerky. Normally, she never passed it up. Sunday had an appetite with the best of them, but not today. She just lay stretched out on the ground near the gas station's back wall.

It wasn't easy for Milt to think of names for dogs. "No, not like an ice cream sundae," Milt would explain to people who asked. The mistake was easy to make. The dog's white coat with spots of brown and black could be likened to vanilla ice cream with hot fudge and a caramel drizzle.

That wasn't what she'd been named after, though. He'd named the dog Sunday after his favorite day of the week. Sunday was Milt's only day off, after all.

He held a piece of beef jerky in front of her, but she didn't respond. "Here you go, girl!" he said, but the dog only stared past him. Milt wondered if she was sick. He looked her over and soon discovered the spots of blood around Sunday's mouth, and the small bit in front of the dog, a strange dark-streaked piece of bloody meat on which the dog had apparently been chewing.

"Okay, looks like you already had your lunch today." Milt dismissed the issue. Over the next few days he wondered, however, when she never seemed to eat another bite and no longer reacted to his voice.

Something *had* to be wrong with that dog. Maybe she was sick.

A gooey film coated her eyes, Milt noticed. This worried him, but as much as he enjoyed the company of the dogs, he didn't have the money to take Sunday to a vet. He ran inside to fetch a paper towel and came back out to moisten it under the gas station's outdoor faucet.

Wiping gently with the wet towel, he cleaned the mess from Sunday's eyes. Underneath, her eyes had changed. They were a bright yellow.

The dog remained distant for days. Over the next month, Sunday never ate anymore, not that Milt saw, but she had to be eating something, even if it remained a complete mystery to him. She had thinned and taken on a sickly appearance. She seldom moved at all. The other dogs stayed away from her, Milt noticed, and his efforts to nurture Sunday proved useless.

His attempts lessened, but he kept trying until one Saturday, Sunday exploded in a fury. Milt screamed as Sunday tore into his wrist, dragged him down with an unbelievable surge of strength, and with vicious jaws wide open, went for his throat.

STRANGER IN THE HAZE

I

"And they said disco was dead."

This was Nadia's murmured answer to the rhythmic thumping from the speakers within one of the smaller clubs lining Candle Square. Smoke swirled around her lithe form as she pressed through a nicotine fog toward the bar.

He sat on a barstool, facing away from her. If he noticed her approach, he gave no indication.

"Who's that at the bar?" she had asked others more than once, but no one knew him. He had seemed so familiar to Nadia before. Who was he?

He faced the bar with no drink in front of him. She reached forward to touch him on the shoulder.

"Nadia," she introduced over the continued disco-pulse. She didn't dare give her last name. When he turned toward her, her heart leaped into her throat.

"Harold," she gasped.

He was different, but it was *him*. He was thin, much too thin, and his pallid skin stretched tightly around the bones of his face. His eyes were a startling yellow.

The memories of her brother-in-law's disappearance flooded back in, and the bloody mess left behind with it. Nadia's husband had been devastated. He hadn't been the same by any stretch since the death—the *perceived* death, so certain until now.

But he sat here, right in front of her, alive.

He smiled. The smile was nothing more than a mechanical curve of his cracked lips. When he stood, she took a fearful step back.

He extended his hand. She gulped, but after a moment of hesitation, she took it. He led her through the crowd and out of the hazy club.

"Harold?" she breathed as he led her farther along, away from the club. She resisted only slightly. Really, it was no resistance at all, and she knew it in the distant, clouded back of her mind.

Words strayed beyond her reach. Everything seemed surreal between her liquor daze and Harold's unnatural reappearance, but she found a sense of exhilaration in the fresh air outside the noise of the club's stifling environment.

He led her across the damp streets and cut through the expanse of Summerset Park. The fresh scent of blooming lilacs brushed Nadia's senses. Soon they crossed to the opposite end of the park, onto another street, and then to another until Nadia lost her sense of direction. They skirted a darkened gas station and turned down the street that was, at the moment, only vaguely familiar to Nadia. They entered the driveway of the abandoned home, vacant since Harold's disappearance, and he pulled her into the house.

In its bedroom, he leaned near, and she breathed in his scent, familiar but touched with the unknown, and before she realized what was happening, they had undressed and she lost her inhibitions on the rough mattress.

The burning surge brought a scream. Her blind pleasure became forgotten in the agonizing aftermath. She thrashed on the bed.

She fought him and shoved him away. He tumbled in the sheets, motionless. She prodded him. He was frigid to the touch.

Nadia screamed again. She stumbled out of the bed and across the floor. Her mind swirled with confusion and fear. She somehow made her way through the home's kitchen, and next she knew, she ran through the streets.

She pounded at a familiar red door.

"Nadia!"

From outside the palisade of delirium her husband's distant voice called to her again and again, but she collapsed to her knees on the floor, swaying.

Her stomach lurched. Within seconds, she fell over, and her cheek met the carpet.

"Nadia!" Her name echoed through her consciousness one last time before everything faded.

II

The fever raged. Nadia's only movement came in an occasional toss or shiver. Soft cries sometimes escaped her lips.

The weeks passed, becoming months.

Nadia fought her way to the light. When she reached it, it struck pain through her and shocked her with its blinding glare.

She was conscious, but it was difficult for her to focus. A dark-featured man stood at her bedside. After a few seconds, she recognized her husband. Another figure, a doctor she decided, was in the room, speaking, but she couldn't understand any of it.

Consciousness left her again. The light slipped from her grasp. She pushed again toward that light, unpleasant as it had been, because that single glimpse of it had fueled her. She wanted to see her husband again, and she wanted to know: what had happened to her? Why was she here?

When she returned to consciousness, her husband was leaning over her. When she moved and tried to speak, he took her warm hands in his own and leaned near.

"Nadia," he whispered. She stared up at him, confused.

"James? Where am I?"

"You're in the hospital. You've been out for a long time." Something seemed strange and dissonant in his words. She dismissed it as a product of residual fever delirium.

"How long?" she asked, her mind filled with fog.

"Months."

"Months? I—I don't believe it. I'm so sorry."

"You're all right now. You've been comatose, but they could never find a reason for it. They couldn't find anything wrong with you at all, Nadia, except for the constant fever, and then it just went away last night."

It was a curious, plastic sympathy in his tone. She saw a strange hardness in his eyes.

"Aren't you happy I'm okay?" she asked, bewildered. When he didn't reply, her eyes turned glassy. Her emotions churned. "What's wrong? Is there something I should know?"

"You're pregnant."

"I'm having a baby?" She went speechless. How was it possible? She couldn't find the words to respond to her husband, a man unable to father children, as a piercing pair of yellow eyes penetrated the murk of her memory.

III

Detective Corbin dialed his partner's number. He allowed the phone to ring several times before finally hanging up the phone.

In the McCullough household, Sandra ignored the ringing. When Brandt McCullough came in the front door a few minutes later, Sandra tossed her beauty magazine onto the coffee table and stood.

"I'm going to bed," she said, and walked toward the bedroom.

McCullough paused just inside the home's front door. "Is everything okay?"

"Everything's just fine," Sandra said. "Nina's asleep. I'm tired. Try not to make too much noise." She shut the bedroom door behind her.

McCullough sighed and fell onto the couch. Whatever was wrong, Sandra wasn't going to address it; therefore, McCullough didn't know what to address. For now, he read over the funnies section of the newspaper. He usually saved that section for last. It helped him wind down after a long day of work. He needed it tonight, but the funny papers weren't that funny today. He felt uncomfortable in his own home, and he hadn't found humor in much lately. This Chambers case was killing him.

In the bedroom, Sandra tossed in the sheets. Her agitation kept her awake, thinking, quietly fuming. Her eyes roamed to Nina's crib in the dark.

They had a child now. Didn't Brandt realize that? Didn't he recognize that things had changed? Didn't he see that he needed to change, or else…

Sandra sighed. She rolled over. Her eyes moved from the crib to the ceiling. In the living room, the telephone rang.

McCullough set down the newspaper and picked up the phone. "McCullough," he answered.

"This is Corbin," Corbin said. "We're at the Chambers house. I know it's late, but you need to come down here."

McCullough's interest perked. "What? Why?"

"It's better if you see this for yourself."

Minutes later, McCullough drove through the night, back to downtown St. Charles, to the house once owned by Harold Chambers. Blue lights colored the front property. Corbin met McCullough at the front door and led him wordlessly to the bedroom, where McCullough laid stunned eyes on the sprawled skeleton in the bed.

IV

Nadia's abdomen swelled over the months. The fever had retreated deep inside. She could feel the burn of the fetus, searing and terrible, just like that night months ago.

"What are you going to name it?" he had asked.

It. James failed to strain the bitterness from his tone.

"Lilac," Nadia said. A harsh laugh escaped James, and he left the room.

After that point, James came and went, but words seldom passed between the couple. She never spoke to him of her encounter with his brother, Harold's strange transformation, or her affair with him. James never asked. He never said much of anything.

He didn't tell his wife about the visit from the police, or his brother's confirmed death. When Detective Corbin showed up at his house to ask questions, he sat drinking and answering Corbin with concise answers that betrayed an edged state of mind.

While the growing fetus burned inside Nadia, the vodka burned in her husband's gut most hours of every day. Behind his toxic silence, rage flared in bloodshot eyes. The loss of his brother had pushed him to the edge, and his wife's obvious betrayal left him teetering on the brink.

He sat in his recliner with the vodka at his side. He stared at the television, but his mind was elsewhere. He thought about the divorce that would come once the baby was here, and then his mind wandered into a far darker place.

He hated it, though it had not yet been born. He hated the child and he hated his wife. He hated his life.

One punch to her abdomen would end it all. One punch, as hard as he could, would send that child straight to Hell where it belonged.

Over the days, James sank further into the mire of his hatred-laced murderous daydreams, and the time for the baby's arrival drew nearer. *Lilac,* that's what she was going to name the thing, as if it was some kind of flower, a thing of beauty. It was an utter lie.

"I don't think it deserves a name," James thought aloud. He looked over to the sofa where Nadia rested. She was oblivious. He told himself that he didn't really care if she heard the previous statement or not. In truth, he hoped she had.

It came on a Tuesday. In a white hospital room, Nadia screamed in the throes of her labor. The pain ignited with renewed fire as it struggled to be free.

Her husband sat alone in their home, watching television and drinking vodka as always, even during his wife's ordeal in the hospital miles away. When the phone's ring broke into the stillness, he ignored it. It persisted until he snatched it from the receiver. At ten-forty-one, Tuesday night, the news came. His wife had died in childbirth, and he was now a father.

1993

POISONED SEED

I

S he resembled no girl he had ever seen. Her appearance brought to mind the image of a starved piranha. Yes, little Lilac Chambers was everything James had expected.

"She doesn't fit," her aunt had pleaded over the phone. "She doesn't fit in anywhere, or with anyone. Please help me."

James got a laugh out of this. "So what?"

"Please, James."

James hung up the phone.

Adoption had been one option, but Nadia's sister had volunteered to take the baby. Without hesitation, James had given his consent.

In those days of Lilac's childhood, the woman seemed to age more rapidly than ever before.

James hadn't fared much better in his solitude. Ruined by the past, James was a man whose life was now behind him.

It had been many years since the day of Nadia's death. James wasn't there. No matter how many more years went by and how long he continued to live in the past, he would never be able to change it. He had hated her so much for what she had done, but he hated himself after it was all over. What could be done about it now? Somewhere in the turmoil of it all, James opened his door to the child.

Following the death of her aunt, young Lilac stood in the doorway. She was a sickly child, frail and pallid, with disheveled black hair and devilish yellow eyes.

"Come on in," he said without emotion. He walked out of the room, the door left open for her while he went to the liquor cabinet to make himself another drink. When he returned with a vodka tonic in hand, she stood inside, looking around and soaking in the sight of her new home. Those yellow eyes turned back to him.

James stared at her without a word. He took another gulp of his drink. "You have a room," he finally said, and walked away. She followed him across the living room to the adjoining hallway. He gestured toward the small bedroom at its end. "There it is."

"Thanks, *daddy.*" James flinched at the word. He whirled on her and released a harsh breath.

"Don't you ever call me that again." His words dripped with newfound venom. His venom came to a boil when he saw the hint of a smile on her lips.

"Get out of my sight," he said through clenched teeth. He turned his back to her and went to the kitchen.

Why had he taken her in? Was his shame so unbearable that he found it easier to deal with the hatred? He couldn't fathom his own decision, but he regretted it.

James often drenched his days in vodka and lived on frozen TV dinners, but over the week following Lilac's arrival, the vodka ran out more often, which meant more trips to the liquor store. The refrigerator remained full of the usual frozen entrees, but James soon noticed that Lilac never touched a single one.

She never seemed to eat anything, period. James wondered if she was even human. Every time he looked at her eyes, he questioned it doubly so.

Some days, she watched inane shows or cartoons, or even a televised circus act as she was currently— mindless television programming. Sometimes she let out a giggle. Other times, she just stared.

"Ladies and gentlemen, boys and girls, welcome to Sutterfield's Circus of the Fantastic!" the television blared. A large man in a ridiculous purple outfit, which included a matching top hat, moved around on a stage.

"Today we bring you the story of John Sutterfield, founder of Sutterfield's Circus of the Fantastic," spoke the local television reporter. "From his humble beginnings in St. Charles nearly twenty years ago, Mr. Sutterfield has taken his show to audiences around the country—"

"I want to go to the circus," Lilac said.

"You *what?*" James asked, caught off-guard.

"I said I wanted to go to the circus." She turned her head, just enough for him to see her yellow eyes.

James snorted. "You belong in a circus." He stood and left the room, found his bottle of vodka, and dove straight to its bottom.

Lilac went back to watching local news coverage of the circus. Somewhere in the audience, watching the televised circus, was off-duty detective Brandt McCullough.

II

"Good show, John. Every bit as good as twenty years ago, if not better."

McCullough sipped bourbon with his old friend, John Sutterfield himself, ringmaster and founder of

Sutterfield's Circus of the Fantastic. The circus had well since closed down for the night.

Sutterfield was an imposing sight to some. He was a large man, both tall and heavyset. His style of dress, the purple tailored suit, made him an unmistakable figure in any crowd.

At McCullough's comment, Sutterfield gave a chuckle and threw back his own glass of twelve-year old bourbon. "The show *is* better, Brandt. I've had that whole twenty years to work on it. You can't tell me it's the damned same after all this time. We were on television tonight, you know."

"Finally got your moment in the spotlight I guess, then," McCullough said after another sip of bourbon. "About ready to retire then?"

Sutterfield sputtered, nearly choking on his drink. "Retire!" he exclaimed.

"No shame in retiring, John."

"Why on earth would I ever retire from the circus? From putting on one hell of a show? It's what I do best."

"You know I'm only a few years from retirement myself," McCullough said, "and we're close enough to the same age. Is retirement really that much of an awful thing?"

"What would I do if I retired?" Sutterfield asked. "Sit around and watch TV? Watch somebody else run my circus?"

"Okay, okay," McCullough said. "I got it. No retirement for John Sutterfield, ever."

"Damned right," Sutterfield asserted. He leaned back in his seat and leaned over to grab the bottle. "So what are you going to do after *you* retire in a few years?" He poured himself another drink and held out the bottle to refill McCullough's glass.

"Do a bit of traveling?" McCullough ventured. "Go out and see the rest of the world?" He shrugged.

"Travel where?" Sutterfield asked. "And see what? I've traveled all around, but I always come back here, because there's no other place like it to me. It's home. My roots are here, in St. Charles."

"I guess mine are, too."

"You guess? You have friends and family here."

McCullough was silent. Sutterfield immediately realized where he'd gone wrong, but it was too late. He'd already said it.

McCullough hadn't known what was coming until it was too late. Losing his marriage was hard, but losing his daughter in the custody battle had been worse. If only McCullough had seen it earlier—but he hadn't. Sandra was gone, and she had taken Nina.

What could he have changed, though? Himself? McCullough took a drink of bourbon and shook away the reflections, which were futile, not to mention crushing when he continued to dwell on them.

"Family?" McCullough said, when he finally did speak. "You mean Nina, or does that even count, considering I'm not allowed to see her?"

"Look, I'm sorry," Sutterfield amended. "I didn't mean to bring it up. You do have friends here, though, and that's not going to change. You grew up here. We both did. That's all I'm saying. It's home. Right?"

"Gotcha," McCullough replied, but the underlying tone was sullen. Sutterfield held out his glass. McCullough's own glass clinked against it, and both men downed their glasses of bourbon.

III

To James, Lilac Chambers represented everything he hated about his life. She was the sum of everything he had lost. Occasionally, he could see the glimmer of a sardonic smile on her face, as though she knew this and took satisfaction in it. Whenever they exchanged words, it was a sour affair.

"Have you been getting into my vodka?" James demanded one day after finding a bottle he didn't remember finishing.

"You drank it," Lilac said.

"Don't play games with me, you little bitch."

"What games?" she asked with a tone of innocence and a smile like acid. "You're a drunk."

Furious, James flung the empty bottle against the wall. Glass rained everywhere. A sharp piece stung his cheek.

"Damn it!" He touched his cheek and felt blood. Lilac giggled. She turned to go back to her room, and James found himself going after her. He grabbed her shoulder. She stopped, but didn't turn back to face him.

James clenched his fist and drew it back. His arm shook with rage, but a tiny glimmer of reason pierced his mind. Did he really want to go to prison for striking a child?

He lowered his fist and released her. She continued the walk into her room without a word, shutting the door. James stood in the hallway, taking deep breaths until he could put a rein on his anger.

He stared at the broken glass littering the carpet. He was in no mood to clean it up right now. Let *her* clean it up, he thought. He went to the bathroom, grabbed the rubbing alcohol, and swabbed some of it over the cut on his cheek. He slammed the bottle of rubbing alcohol down on the counter and left for the liquor store.

When he awoke the following day, he felt sick. His head throbbed like it might detonate at any second. Every day, he felt worse than the day before. Today, he could barely muster the ability to roll out of bed. He could swear that little girl was poisoning him. Her presence in the house was poisonous enough.

In the bathroom, he noticed the bottle of isopropyl alcohol from the previous day. The bottle was almost empty. His eyes narrowed. His sludgy mind worked in unison with his sour stomach.

She was sitting on the sofa when James walked into the living room. The sight of her made him feel more ill. Without acknowledging her presence, he sat in his recliner and watched the television.

He felt awful. Maybe it would pass within a few hours, but he doubted he would be able to accomplish anything today. He swore under his breath.

She was watching him. When their eyes met, she stood and went to her room again. James sat in silence. His mind swirled until the vodka and almost-empty bottle of rubbing alcohol slammed together in his jumbled thoughts.

She *was* poisoning him.

"She wants me to die." His anger vanished, and a cold grasp of the truth remained.

He stood up, walked to the hallway, and he threw the door to her room open. She stood in front of her bed, staring at him, but didn't appear surprised and didn't back away. She scarcely put up a struggle when he grabbed her throat with both hands and squeezed with all of his strength.

IV

With the car's headlights turned off, he slowed along the gravel road and pulled off to one side. He climbed out, walked around to the trunk, and sprang it open. He lifted Lilac's body from it and carried her across the creaky old bridge. He threw her over the side and watched her vanish into the dark ravine.

"That's it," he whispered, about the closest thing that came to mind for a eulogy.

The drive home was peaceful. James felt as if a tremendous burden was lifted from his life. He went into the kitchen and threw a frozen dinner in the microwave. When he sat again in his living room recliner, he didn't even feel the need for a drink.

In his night's sobriety, the house was quiet. *Of course it's quiet,* he thought, but it seemed even more so than he could ever remember.

"What's wrong with me?" he muttered. "Maybe I'll have that drink after all." He made it a short distance, and stopped in front of the hallway. He looked toward her bedroom door. The full realization of what he had done only seeped through him, but—*it felt like she was still here.*

He had killed her, hadn't he? If the initial act hadn't done so, the fall into the ravine would have. She was dead. She had to be. He looked into her bedroom, and as expected, it was empty.

What was it, then? He had heard nothing of anyone discovering the girl's body yet. Then again, hadn't it only been hours?

He began to drink again. The vodka didn't quell his nerves this time. The discomfort outweighed everything he did to distract himself. There was only one thing left to do.

James drove back out to the bridge. He looked around to make certain he wasn't seen by anyone, and took the flashlight from the passenger's seat. He climbed out of the car, switched on the flashlight, and walked to the end of the bridge to peer over the edge.

He shone the flashlight into the ravine. He looked for a few minutes, but couldn't see her body; the bottom of the ravine was some distance down, and it was too difficult to see. He would have to climb down. There wasn't any other way he could be sure.

He heard the noise of a twig snapping somewhere in the dark unseen. His heart jumped. The prospect of going down into the ravine gave way to fear. He turned the flashlight in the direction of the sound, but saw nothing, and that's when he felt the shove.

He cried out. Above, he saw a face so white it might have been painted, like that of a clown. It watched him fall.

James flailed down through the darkness. The ravine engulfed him, and so did unconsciousness.

James stirred. He tried to move, but it was impossible. A bone jutted from one arm. His legs were broken. He struggled to breathe and wheezed for oxygen.

His body sprawled among the rocks at the bottom of the ravine. He saw her, not far away. Her breathing was faint, but she *was* breathing, and she moved.

Her eyes opened, the pure yellow irises burning into him. "I knew you would come back eventually, *daddy.*"

A poisonous smile crept across her lips.

THE RIDE

The sunlight of early morning filtered down. On the ground in front of her, a body lay motionless. Satisfied, she stood and began her climb out of the rocky ravine.

Though her ordeal had weakened her, she felt good. She no longer felt the emptiness that always seemed on the brink of swallowing her. From the beginning, the poison had been inside her, with the bleak choice to either fight against it and tear herself to shreds or to embrace it.

As she grew through the years, it had remained in infancy, feeding on her and leaving her an undernourished child at the best of times. Now, everything had changed. She had been near death, and she had felt it drawing on the remaining life in her, the only way for it to sustain itself. When *he* had come along, it had drawn on *his* life, and in some way, so had she.

That tiny poisoned seed began to grow.

The climb out of the ravine took several minutes. Once back on the gravel road, she began to walk. Her steps quickened. She rode the flow of the powerful immensity that became her. She ran.

Charlie's eyes widened in surprise. He punched the brakes. Something had streaked right by him, he could swear it! He craned his head to look out the window of his pickup truck and scanned the roadside and the trees of the surrounding wooded area.

There was no sign of anything that might have been the black-and-white blur. It had to be his imagination. If so, his imagination had startled him.

He allowed his hands to rest on the wheel for a few seconds, and glanced at the green apple resting in the passenger's seat. It was one of the fresh-picked ones from the orchard. He picked it up in one hand. With the other, he flicked open the glove compartment and grabbed his old fishing knife, which would suffice as a paring knife.

He cut a slice from the apple and chewed it. It was soft, sweet and juicy, a nice little quick snack. He took his time, eating another couple of apple slices before he flung what was left into the glove compartment and began driving again. The battered old pickup bumped over the road of dirt and gravel.

After driving a few more minutes, he saw the girl walking on the side of the road. His first instinct was to push on, but relaxed his foot on the gas pedal when it occurred to him that he couldn't leave a young girl out here in the middle of nowhere, where anything might happen.

"Need a ride?" he called out the truck's window. The girl looked up. Charlie's mouth fell open.

Her eyes were yellow and sunken in her gaunt features. Her dark hair was a mess. Charlie tried to put aside his shock. He forced a smile, and to his surprise, the girl gave him a weary smile back.

"Thanks," she said. "A ride would be good." Charlie unlocked the passenger's side door for her, and she climbed in.

"You doing okay?" Charlie asked her. She gave a nod.

"So what's a youngster like you doing way out here?" Charlie asked once they were moving down the road. He tried to keep a casual note, but could scarcely disguise his interest. She looked at him for a moment, and turned her head back to look at the road.

"Just walking," she said. "I'm not old enough to drive."

He gave a nervous chuckle. "Charlie," he introduced. When she didn't respond, he prompted her further. "What's your name?"

"Lilac," she answered.

"I've never heard that name before," Charlie said. She didn't answer. Charlie decided on a straightforward approach. "Do you need to go to the hospital?"

"No." She winced. Charlie watched this curious reaction from the corner of his eye. His mind churned. Should he take her to the hospital anyway? Or was she a runaway? Should he go to the police?

Lilac slumped against the door of the truck. Alarmed, Charlie shook her. Her face was pale, but her strange eyes were open.

His mind was made up. Charlie would take her straight to the hospital. Whatever was wrong with her, she needed help *soon*.

He pressed down on the accelerator, shifting his gaze between Lilac and the road. He flung open the glove compartment and shoved his fishing knife aside to grab what remained of the apple. He held it out to her.

"Here, you need to eat something," he said urgently. She looked at it for a few seconds, and took it in her hands with a lethargic motion.

"Eat," Charlie told her after she stared at the fruit for several seconds.

"I can't eat this," she said.

"Try," he said. "You need to eat something." He paused. "I'm taking you to the hospital." Despite her condition, her brow furrowed and her eyes sharpened.

"I already told you. I don't need to go to the hospital."

"Okay," he replied. "But eat something, that's all I ask, at the very least."

Lilac hesitated. She held the apple to her lips. With obvious reluctance, she took a bite and chewed it carefully.

"Good," Charlie encouraged, glad to see the girl take some nourishment. She didn't want to go to the hospital, but he planned on taking her there, regardless. He just hoped he could get her there in time. He would do everything he could, he promised himself.

He almost jumped out of his skin when Lilac vomited into the floorboard. Blood and apple chunks splashed around her feet. Charlie's heart thumped like a locomotive. He braked and whipped the truck off to one side of the road.

He took her by the shoulder. She continued to heave, but nothing else came out. "I told you," she sputtered. "I told you!"

"Are you—are you all right?"

"I can't keep it down." Lilac took a deep, shuddering breath. "I never could. My aunt tried to feed me when I was a lot younger. It just made me sicker."

"Your aunt?" Charlie questioned. "Where does your aunt live?"

"She doesn't." Lilac entered a violent coughing fit. She slumped against the truck door again.

Charlie opened the glove compartment again and searched it in vain for something that might help. He saw nothing but the papers on his truck and the rusted fishing knife.

Lilac's breathing slowed and began to stabilize. Weakly, her head turned to look down at the opened glove compartment. Her lips parted, and her expression twisted. Charlie reached out to close the glove compartment, but the fishing knife was in Lilac's hand.

The rusty metal blade tore through his throat. Charlie gurgled a scream. His blood sprayed against the truck's windshield.

Lilac sat upright, her recovery immediate. She sighed with a thought of the body she had left back in the ravine. She had felt better then, and now she was elevated to a new height of ecstasy—of power.

Beside her, Charlie twitched.

She ran her fingers through her blood-streaked hair and climbed out of the truck. She tucked the fishing knife into one pocket, stepped onto the road again, and resumed walking, not running, to conserve that curious reserve of power within. Some change had befallen her at the bottom of that ravine, she now knew for certain, but she had tested her new boundaries too quickly last time. She could do without another round of sickness.

Charlie's truck had vanished into the distance behind her when the next vehicle, a four-door sedan, stopped beside her.

"Hey," the driver called. "Do you need a ride?"

ONE MAN'S PRICE

I

Jacob Pennington rose earlier than most. He had his typical breakfast of two boiled eggs sliced in half, dry toast, and coffee. For years, he had eaten the same breakfast every day, and had seldom deviated from his routines. Today, when he went outside to check the mail, his life changed.

A large, padded manila envelope, with no return address marked, sat in his mailbox. Cash lined the inside of the envelope. His eyes widened.

He counted the money. "My word," he whispered. "Ten thousand dollars!"

He unfolded the accompanying letter, hands trembling. *I have watched you,* it read in a child-like scrawl, and in orange crayon, no less. *I know you'll accept this, in return for the following arrangements…*

He read over it several times. His mind raced. The letter's sender remained unknown, but the words on the paper were as crystal-clear as the money was green.

There is more where this came from, the final words of the letter read. Pennington counted the money again.

He glanced at his watch. It was almost time to head to work. Work? He had ten thousand dollars in his hands right now.

He stopped and took a deep breath. "Don't lose your cool," he chastised himself. He read the letter one more time. Once Pennington made his choice, he knew there would be no turning back.

He took the money, climbed into his police cruiser, and left. For Officer Jacob Pennington, the manila envelope, containing the cash and that simple folded letter, would only be the first of many.

II

Thunder rumbled in a gray sky. The rain came down in a steady drizzle. After throwing back the remainder of a cup of Corbin's awful coffee, for the caffeine if nothing else, McCullough jumped out of the car. He and Corbin, already wearing yellow raincoats to guard against the coming storm, approached the truck. Officers Pennington and Watkins were already there, also dressed in raincoats, inspecting the driver's side area of the truck.

The man's face was against the glass, his throat open in a grotesque red grin. Dried blood dotted the driver's side window and caked the inside of the windshield.

McCullough and Corbin exchanged glances. Corbin opened his mouth to speak, and the second call came in.

Another body had been found out by the old bridge. Pennington drew a sharp breath.

"I'll go," McCullough said. Without delay, he hopped into the unmarked vehicle and took off for the bridge.

McCullough sped down the gravel road for a few minutes, until he saw the old wooden bridge ahead and the patrol cars near it. He stopped short of the bridge and pulled off to the side, in front of the ravine. He applied the emergency brake and climbed out. An officer on the scene met him and directed him toward the ravine's bottom, where the others had gathered.

McCullough began the arduous climb down the steep decline. After a few minutes, he reached the ravine's bottom and approached the body.

When he was able to make out the face, he halted in his tracks. Fear rippled through his spine. It was the second dead man he had seen in the span of a few minutes. The face wasn't even recognizable as a human's. There was only a bloody, deformed mess. The face and skull had been brutally bashed in. Half-buried in the mud beside him was a large rock covered with his dried blood, the instrument of his death.

The surrounding officers looked to McCullough as he moved closer to examine the man's body. While McCullough puzzled over the body in the ravine, miles away, Corbin continued his own hunt for information at the site of the pickup truck.

Corbin's lips tightened. He moved around to the other side of the truck and inspected the ground on that side. He carefully opened the passenger's side door and scanned the interior. Officers Pennington and Watkins remained nearby. While Corbin's mind worked to process every detail and possible scenario of the truck driver's murder, Pennington's thoughts were elsewhere.

Hours before, in the dark early morning before the official discovery of the truck driver's body, Pennington was here. He had followed the instructions given by his benefactor in the cash-filled manila envelope. Over the course of several minutes, Pennington had worked to clear the killer's tracks in every conceivable way.

Now, a second body had been reported. McCullough was investigating it even now. Before, Pennington had known nothing about a *second* body. What had he gotten himself into?

At the first ghastly sight of the truck driver, Pennington had nearly turned and bolted, but had fought to regain his nerve and come to terms with the motivation that brought him here. In the end, he had carried out his part. It was too late to turn back now.

Ten thousand dollars. Pennington was a step closer to digging his way out of debt. His mysterious benefactor could turn his life around, he realized, but if Pennington tried to change his course now, he might place himself at risk.

Whoever *they* were, they knew who Pennington was, and they knew his weakness, or so it definitely appeared. Pennington, however, knew nothing about them. That gave them a large amount of leverage against him, especially now. If his actions were ever uncovered, his life would be over.

There is more where this came from. He remembered that part of the letter well. He saw no alternative.

This remained on Pennington's mind for much of the day while he went about his duties. He barely noticed at a later hour when McCullough passed him.

On his way out of the department, McCullough nodded to the officer. Pennington nodded back. Something struck McCullough as off-kilter about the officer's demeanor today.

A sixth sense, or just a false alarm inside my head? Probably the latter, McCullough reasoned, with the events of late. The recent deaths had them all tense. *Surely that's what's wrong with me lately. Or is it Nina?*

It had been on his mind again lately, at least until the bodies were discovered, but he refused to let himself wander down that self-destructive path of thought. He forced himself back to the task at hand.

The body in the ravine was still in question. It had been identified as a Mr. James Chambers. Chambers had a daughter, Lilac Chambers, in his care. She was missing, but they were still searching.

McCullough had another thought of his own daughter. He hadn't seen her in...

Focus, he told himself. *Chambers.*

He thought of the Chambers case from years ago and pondered it on the drive home. He and Corbin had witnessed that gruesome scene firsthand. Who could forget what they found in the home's bedroom sometime after that incident, those skeletal remains lying spread-eagle on the mattress?

He filed it away in his mind for now. He was home. He walked up the stairs to his apartment, the one he had lived in since the divorce.

Bitter memories of that time charred his temperament. He grasped at the one good thing to come of it all, Nina, but she was out of his reach.

He had tried before, more times than he would ever be able to count. He was about to try again.

He picked up the phone, stared at it, and took a breath. He dialed the number.

"Hello?" came the voice, Sandra's voice. McCullough's spirits sank.

"Hello," he said back. "It's me."

"You shouldn't be calling here."

"Is Nina there?"

"She doesn't want to talk to you, Brandt."

"I never hear that from her," McCullough fired, anger biting him. "I only hear it from you."

"She's been through enough already," Sandra launched back. "Haven't we already dragged this through court enough times? Why can't you just leave us alone? You didn't give a damn about Nina or me back when we were married, so why does it matter now?"

"That's a lie, and you know it," McCullough said. In response, he heard a click.

McCullough almost threw the phone, but stopped himself. He started to call back, but paused mid-number. If he called back now, he knew, it would only bring another flood of hurtful words, another shouting match.

He let out a sigh, dropped the phone onto the couch, and decided to go take a shower.

1997

SHOWTIME

I

An older woman's body lay limp in a rocking chair. Blood dripped from her lacerated scalp to the carpeted floor. Across the room, her husband sprawled lifeless on the carpet.

Victims of their own compassion, they never knew.

Lilac walked out the front door and left the dead couple behind. The force inside her satiated, her mind was clear. Her thoughts were on the circus, that wonderful show which intrigued her in her youth and amazed her in her adolescence.

Ladies and gentlemen, boys and girls, welcome to Sutterfield's Circus of the Fantastic!

Her stride quickened with purpose.

Within the same hour, past the River Bridge and Summerset Park, and well beyond Candle Square, Brandt McCullough and C. J. Corbin stood outside the St. Charles Police Department.

"I guess this is it, then," Corbin said.

"I guess so."

"Between the two of us," McCullough said to Corbin, "I think we did some damned fine work."

Corbin nodded his agreement. He extended a hand, which McCullough shook. "Still moving up to Wellville?" Corbin asked.

"Yeah, I think it'll do me some good to get out of town," McCullough said. "I have some good memories here, but there are a lot of bad ones I just can't shake."

A thought of Sandra jumped into his mind. He dispelled it in a hurry. Nina also came into his thoughts, but thinking about the daughter he never came to know didn't help much, either. He sighed.

"I'm sure I'll come around and visit," McCullough said. "It isn't like I'm moving across the country, you know."

"Make sure you do," Corbin said. "And take care of yourself. Good luck with everything."

McCullough walked to his car, climbed in, and drove away, leaving his badge and gun with the St. Charles Police Department. As of today, Brandt McCullough was retired.

He walked up the stairs to his apartment and began packing his belongings. He filled a cardboard box with dishes, packed it with newspaper, and sealed it. He started on another box. He tossed several miscellaneous items into it until he came across a framed picture of Nina at two years of age. She had McCullough's dark hair and eyes, and her mother's nose, small and narrow, and slightly upturned at the end.

As he looked at it, and his wandered down an inevitably dismal avenue, the phone rang.

"Hello?"

"Over two decades and still going strong, here. You've officially lived out your whole career in that time." It was Sutterfield. McCullough chuckled.

"That's mostly true," he admitted. "Even if you're really just being a jackass. My line of work isn't like circus work though, John. You know that."

"Isn't? Don't you mean *wasn't?*"

"Whatever," McCullough dismissed. "So I take it you're calling to invite me to *your* retirement party now?"

"I'll never retire!" Sutterfield declared. "I'll be doing this till I'm old and gray!"

"That was a few years ago, John."

"I'll be doing it till I'm dead and buried, then."

"I believe you. You're a persistent bastard."

Sutterfield snorted. "So are you still leaving town?"

"I was packing when you called. I've still got a lot of work ahead of me here."

"Don't get in too much of a hurry," Sutterfield said. "I've got a show going on tonight. You ought to come out one last time before you leave St. Charles. How about it?"

"I'm getting a little old for the circus."

"You've got to be kidding. That's no excuse. Look at me!"

"Yeah. Okay, I'll agree with that."

"Wait a minute. What's that supposed to mean?"

McCullough stifled a laugh. "Nothing at all. I'll be there."

A lot of people didn't know what it meant having a circus fiend for a friend, McCullough guessed. He got off the phone, and spent the rest of the day clearing out his apartment.

II

"Ladies and gentlemen, boys and girls, welcome to Sutterfield's Circus of the Fantastic! Tonight the impossible will pass right in front of your eyes! Witness man versus beast, here on stage! See the Master of the Blades and his deadly hundred whirling knives! Watch Danforth the Illusionist work his magnificent magic! That, and much, much more! It's all happening right here, right now, in Sutterfield's Circus of the Fantastic! Let the show begin!" The large man in purple, wearing his matching purple top hat, left the stage.

The audience cheered. John Sutterfield just couldn't seem to resist mentioning himself in the third person, Brandt McCullough noted from somewhere among the stands, even after all these years. He had to admit, though, that John had done what few ever accomplished: he had lived out his childhood dream.

The Master of the Blades took the stage first. With expert precision the man flung each blade, each with increasing distance. Every knife struck its mark. McCullough almost felt sorry for the poor girl holding the wooden target up, but the Master of the Blades proved flawless in his efforts. The danger was a mere part of the act, and the girl faced no actual danger at all.

McCullough's gaze meandered. His eyes passed over several others in the crowd, including the dark-haired teenage girl several rows away, who watched the act intensely. An unexpected brief round of nausea distracted him, but he managed to get it under control, and when his stomach settled, he looked back to the stage. The show went on.

When the closing act came down and the stands began to clear, John Sutterfield and the rest of the performers cleaned up backstage. The Master of the Blades, Jackson, was careful in his packing items away, while nearby, his assistant haphazardly flung small stage props into a box. He glanced over and saw the irritation on her features, and it was not difficult for him to guess the source.

"You're doing good work out there," Jackson reassured her. "Don't listen to Emerson. This isn't his act, anyway."

"Yeah, I thought tonight's show was pretty cool," Susie replied. "I don't know what his problem is. I can't stand him."

Jackson was tall, especially next to the younger girl. Though slender, Jackson's body rippled with muscles, physically fine-tuned by the rigors of his longtime role as Master of the Blades. Susie, his assistant, was a red-headed girl of nineteen.

"Don't let Emerson run you off," Jackson told her, continuing to pack. "Just ignore him. There isn't much else you can do. If he didn't pull his own, Sutterfield would have gotten rid of him a long time ago. Everybody wants to see the Alligator Man, though. It's one of our main attractions, in St. Charles, at least."

"I don't like the way he treats the animals, either," Susie added.

"What I don't know—"

"But you *do* know, Jackson! Don't pretend like you don't." Susie turned fully to face Jackson, her face flushed in frustrated anger. "I should go to Sutterfield about that bastard."

"Don't think other people haven't," Jackson replied. "You're probably just going to make things worse though, Susie."

"Maybe I don't care." She walked out. Jackson released an audible sigh of exasperation as she left the tent.

Susie walked through the cool night, trying to calm herself. The sounds of drunken revelry came from another of the tents, where the circus clowns held another cheap wine-soaked free-for-all bash. Best not to get caught up in that, she thought. A drunken clown stumbled out of the tent. Susie quickened her pace.

When she gained some distance and solitude, she slowed. A gentle breeze soothed her.

She wandered by a cluster of trees, and released a yawn. She stopped and sat down against one of the trees, her back to its rough trunk. She closed her eyes. *Just a moment's rest,* she decided.

In less than a minute, she fell into slumber. While she slept unaware against the tree, a shadow fell across her.

III

"I don't understand," Jackson said. "Things were going so well. And she just left?"

"Apparently," John Sutterfield said. "Nobody's seen her. It looks like you'll have to find another assistant."

"I guess Emerson got to her," Jackson muttered once Sutterfield left. He knew what came next, though. The long, painful process of trying to find another girl brave enough, or stupid enough, according to some, to take part as Jackson's assistant in the ever-anticipated Master of the Blades act. He knew he had to get on the task immediately.

Finding a girl to replace Susie wouldn't be easy. Most girls didn't want to apply for a job as a target on two legs. If only Susie had stuck it out—she had been one of the best so far. She had left because of Emerson, no doubt. The Alligator Man couldn't resist antagonizing people on a regular basis and trying to make Jackson's job more difficult.

Jackson went through a number of potential entrants: Karen, Michelle, Lilac, Amy, Heather. From the pool of part-time assistance the circus had employed, these were the ones who expressed an interest in filling the role. A couple of the girls backed out once they discovered what was involved. He wasn't sure about the others yet, but one of the girls did linger on his mind in a strange sort of way.

Lilac. Those piercing yellow eyes stuck in his mind, and there was some aspect of her character that—well, he wasn't certain, but it was different.

Being memorable was a positive quality, wasn't it? This was the circus, after all. Seldom did the average Joe or Jane have any desire to join its bizarre ranks.

He decided to meet with her again. Only when he presented her with an entrance exam of sorts, as he did with all assistants in the past, could he be certain.

A few minutes after Lilac arrived for her second "interview," her audition, Jackson spotted her at the other end of the tent speaking with Sutterfield's man of magic, Danforth the Illusionist.

"You're Jackson's new girl, huh?" Danforth the Illusionist asked her.

Without his circus attire, colored handkerchiefs, fluttering black and white birds, magic hat, and fireworks, Dan wasn't a figure to stand out in a crowd. He was a quiet, somewhat shy individual of slight figure, and shorter than Lilac.

"I don't know yet."

"Oh."

"I love the circus, though. I hope I get the job."

"Good luck."

"Thank you," she said.

"I'm Dan," he said.

"Lilac." She cocked her head slightly. "Are you Danforth the Illusionist? That's what they call you on stage, isn't it? I've seen your act."

He laughed nervously. "Off the stage, I'm just Dan."

"I really liked your act."

"Sorry to break this up," Jackson interrupted with a friendly pat on Dan's back, "but it's time. Come on, Lilac. I'll show you what we're up against."

As he led the black-haired girl away, he again detected that unusual quality about her, one he couldn't quite place. Then again, he reminded himself, maybe that made her right for the circus.

They were outside now. Jackson arranged the larger standing targets and handed Lilac one of the smaller, portable ones. He set up the gray metal foldout stand and set a duffel bag beneath it. On top of the stand he laid his collection of knives, designed for perfect balance in throwing.

"The first part of the act is done with large, standing targets. After that, you'll be holding the smaller targets. The crowd loves it. It puts them on the edge of their seats. Watch."

Jackson spun around and hurled the knife. It thudded into the standing target's bulls-eye. He picked up two more knives, one in each hand, and threw them simultaneously to strike a double bulls-eye.

"Now watch this," Jackson said. He snatched another knife from the table and flung it, whirled to grab another blade with his other hand and sent that one through the air, then another, and became a tornado of rapid motion. A volley of knives riddled the target to outline the bulls-eye in a circle.

"You're unbelievable," Lilac whispered.

"That's called the 'hundred whirling knives,'" Jackson told her, "even though there aren't actually a hundred knives. I didn't name it that, the fans of the show did."

"You were great on stage, but from this close, it's even more incredible," Lilac said.

Jackson removed each of the knives from the target and returned them to the table. "Now," he said to Lilac, "I want you to walk over there and hold that target out for me."

"Like this?" She stood next to the standing target and held the smaller portable target out at arm's length.

"That's good," Jackson replied. "I'm going to throw this blade into the target you're holding. Are you okay?"

"Yes. Go ahead."

Interesting, Jackson thought. No fear and no hesitation.

Jackson drew back the knife and let it sail. It smacked into the target point-first and center. Jackson had to admire the way the girl handled it. She didn't even flinch. Even Susie had been shaky the first time, but it didn't even phase this new girl.

She held two targets for the next practice round. Jackson hit them both with a double throw. Next, he retrieved the duffel bag from beneath the table and brought out the throwing axe.

"You'll need to hold the target with both hands this time," Jackson instructed her. "Right in front of you." She complied. *Brave girl,* Jackson thought. He raised the axe, and hurled it toward its mark. The heavy blade cartwheeled through the air and struck the wooden target. Despite the force, she didn't buckle, or even move at all.

Yes, Jackson thought. *She'll do nicely.*

"Welcome to the Sutterfield's Circus of the Fantastic," he said, unable to suppress a smile.

IV

The practice sessions ensued and continued through the week in preparation for the coming performance. Lilac, while withdrawn at times, remained coordinated, focused, and strong.

She was the best assistant Jackson remembered having. Susie was in the past.

He noticed Lilac speaking to Dan on occasion. The magician wasn't particularly outgoing, and neither was Lilac, but the two seemed to have found something in common. What that might be, aside from both sharing a distance from the rest of the performers, Jackson couldn't guess.

The show was tomorrow. Jackson would need his rest. For Lilac, it would be the first real show.

As Jackson headed to bed for the night, in another tent, Danforth the Illusionist reclined and sipped a glass of milk. A plate of crackers with cheese rested beside him. Across the space of his small tent sat Lilac. He held the plate out to offer her some, but she shook her head.

"I can't eat that," she said. "It just makes me sick."

He shrugged and crunched one of them down. He washed it down with another gulp of milk. Lilac watched him.

"What made you join the circus?" she asked.

"I was nobody before I joined the circus," Dan said. "Just a two-bit magician with a few tricks up his sleeve. John Sutterfield took me on board with the circus and showed me to the crowds. If not for him, I would still just be Dan Andrews, the little guy nobody ever heard of or cared about. How about you, Lilac? What made you want to join the circus?"

"I saw the circus on TV when I was younger," she said. "I always wanted to see it in person." She paused, thinking. "Someone told me once that I belonged in the circus. It's almost funny. The circus does seem like the place for someone like me. I've never really fit in anywhere else."

"You're in the right place," Dan said. "I don't think many of us do."

Lilac smiled without mirth.

"They say a good magician never reveals his tricks," Dan said, "but you told me how much you liked my act, and I can't help wanting to show you a little bit of something."

He led her to the back of the tent where multiple stacks of boxes rested and began to open them. Lilac stared at the contents. Dan explained them to her, the thrilling lights and explosions that punctuated his act—the pyrotechnics.

Night turned into morning, and the sun rose to a new day, Friday. John Sutterfield began preparations early. When the rest of the performers were up and about, they joined in the efforts. By midday, everything was ready, and all could enjoy a moment's rest, but the tension remained, as did the excitement.

When the evening hours drew near, that magical word was poised on the lips of John Sutterfield: "Showtime!"

Dan prepared his pyrotechnics, mirrors, and stage illusions. The acrobats stretched and performed their routine warm-up exercises. The clowns applied makeup and outfits in their tent. The rest milled around in their own respective tents. Jackson brought Lilac to his tent, where he counted out his blades.

"Think your new girl's going to be able to handle it?" came a voice from the tent's opening. Jackson looked up. A large man stood under the flap of the tent.

The speaker was William Emerson, the Alligator Man, a giant of a man. Muscles knotted his bulk, and he was taller even than Jackson.

Once, he had been renowned for wrestling alligators as part of his act, where his moniker was derived. The circus didn't transport the alligators while on the road, however, and they were only included in Emerson's act on the special occasions when the show came home to St. Charles.

"She'll be able to do more than 'handle it,' Emerson," Jackson replied. He went back to counting knives. Emerson looked down at Lilac. She stared back at him.

"We'll see," Emerson said. "But if she messes this up—"

Jackson looked up again, this time with irritation. "Get out of here, Emerson," he said. "This is my act. It doesn't have anything to do with you. Worry about yourself."

Emerson opened his mouth as if about to deliver a harsh reply, but stopped short. "We'll see," he repeated under his breath at last, and left the tent.

The show was on. After Sutterfield made his introduction, the circus kicked into full gear. As always, Jackson, Master of the Blades, led the first act. Lilac joined him.

Knives slammed into each of the targets in Lilac's hands. Knives and axes flew, each right on target to the awe of the crowd. Jackson's hundred whirling knives finished the act. Lilac upheld her duties with perfection.

Jackson and Lilac left the spotlight, and act two kicked in. Soon, the opening pyrotechnic display of Danforth the Illusionist crackled overhead while Jackson and Lilac stood backstage.

"Beautiful," Jackson praised Lilac. "Just beautiful. I would like to hear Emerson try to run his mouth now!"

NO ESCAPE

I

There was one part of Lilac that Dan Andrews identified with, a girl lost and misunderstood. It was this side of her he delighted with sleight-of-hand tricks, and this girl who stared with large, attentive eyes when he showed her the myriad of stage pyrotechnics stored in his tent.

The other side of her left him wondering. He saw it in an occasional twist of her expression or an iciness that came into her yellow eyes at random moments. It came with the bouts of silence, when she would not speak to him or anyone else.

Dan noticed the other changes as well, over the following week. The periods of silent strangeness lengthened, and she became more withdrawn. Before long, Dan would rarely even see her, apart from the circus performances.

One night, she came to him without warning. Her features were ashen.

Dan pushed his discomfort aside and welcomed her into his tent. She sat in the proffered seat, but didn't speak.

"What's wrong?" Dan asked her. He flinched at his own directness. "I mean to say, are you okay? You haven't looked well lately. I mean…" He faltered when she looked at him.

After a long pause, she spoke in a murmur. "The older I get, the more it grows. The other part of me. The other me."

"I don't understand, Lilac. What's happening to you?"

"Of course you don't understand. You couldn't." She stood. Dan shrank back into his seat.

"I just want you to be well," was Dan's forced, weak utterance. Lilac approached and stood close in front of him. She gazed down at him with more than a slight gleam in her razor eyes.

Dan's heart pounded. He fought against his spiking fear to find words.

"Jackson can tell," Dan said. "That something is wrong, I mean. Emerson is giving him grief about it. He says you're sick, that you won't be able to keep doing the shows."

"And what do *you* think?" she asked him in a quiet, fathomless tone.

"I don't know." He tensed, uncertain of what to expect. She backed away.

"It's still inside me, Dan. I wondered if the circus could change things for me, but it hasn't changed anything. I can still feel it, and there is no escape."

Dan was floored. "It?"

Before lifting the tent's flap to exit, she said, "The Living Poison."

II

Jackson sat alone after the night's show. He shook his head, distraught, while using a soft white cloth to wipe his blades. When Emerson walked in with a smug grin, Jackson cursed.

"Your girl barely held up through tonight's show, Jackson."

Jackson kept polishing his blades. "I didn't ask for your opinion."

"She ain't got what it takes," Emerson went on, "and if you don't take care of it, I will. Seems to me like you ought to be taking care of your own business, though."

Jackson threw the blade down and stood tall. Emerson's grin widened.

"What are you gonna do about it?" Emerson goaded.

"Turn around and walk away, Emerson," Jackson replied, his tone cool but as edged as his blades.

Emerson's grin vanished. His lips twisted into a sneer. "Come over here and make me, boy."

Jackson strode toward the Alligator Man. Emerson raised his fists. Jackson acknowledged to himself that he had looked forward to this for a long, long time.

The blast of a shotgun rang out. Emerson flinched. Jackson took a step back.

The rotund ringmaster of Sutterfield's Circus of the Fantastic stood in the tent's entrance, his double-barrel shotgun in his hands.

"Now that I have your attention," Sutterfield said, "do you two want to tell me what this is all about? Jackson? Emerson? Anybody?" He gave an exaggerated look around the empty tent.

"Look, Mr. Sutterfield," began Emerson. "I didn't mean no—"

"I was running this show while you were in diapers," he told Emerson. "Don't think for a minute I won't throw you out on your ass. Get out of here." He motioned to the tent's exit with the shotgun. Emerson nodded, but stole one last glare at Jackson before he left.

"It was about your new girl, wasn't it?" Sutterfield asked Jackson. Jackson nodded. Sutterfield sighed. "Look. You're good at what you do. You always have been. You've always put on one hell of a show, and that's what we're all about here. This new girl of yours, though—she has to go. You need to get yourself a new assistant trained before the next show."

Sutterfield walked out, leaving Jackson wondering how he could deliver such news to Lilac. He knew Sutterfield was right, but in the same breath, he knew something was wrong about the circumstances.

The girl was clearly ill in some way. Jackson suspected drugs. This would explain her bizarre attitude and her appearance, which was beginning to resemble a caged carnivore.

He walked across the grounds to Lilac's small tent, the one Jackson had lent her until she could afford her own. He opened the flap and leaned in. "Lilac," he whispered into the dark tent's interior.

After a moment of silence, she answered. What is it?"

"Listen," Jackson said. "I just had a talk with Mr. Sutterfield." He took a deep breath. "Things aren't working out, Lilac. I'm sorry. We have to let you go."

He waited for a response, but nothing came. He opened his mouth to speak again, to urge her to find help for whatever troubled her whether it be drugs or actual physical sickness of some kind, but decided it was not his place to lecture her. He had dismissed her, and that was enough.

He closed the tent's flap, walking away, and decided he could at least allow her to finish out the night's sleep. He returned to his own tent, his head down, his steps slow, and his thoughts gloomy.

In another tent, Dan woke, hearing a sound. Someone had whispered his name, he thought. He climbed out of his cot, threw some clothes on, and walked outside.

Lilac watched him as he emerged. Her hard stare thrust a paralyzing splinter of fear into his gut.

"They let me go, Dan."

Dan blinked. "Really?" He struggled for something to say. "I didn't know. I'm really sorry, Lilac."

She approached him. He took an unconscious step back. She stood near, searching his eyes with her own yellow irises. Her lips parted to speak to him, but another voice interrupted.

"You ain't supposed to be here."

The Alligator Man lumbered toward them. He glared down at Lilac. Like before, she returned his gaze evenly.

"Look, Emerson—" Dan spoke.

"I wasn't talking to you," Emerson said. "I was talking to this little freak who got herself kicked out of the show." He stepped toward her. "What are you still doing here? Do I need to pick you up by your hair and throw you out myself?"

Dan stepped between the two. "We were talking, Emerson. You need to leave her alone."

The large fist crashed into Dan's jaw. The shocked magician reeled backwards and tumbled to the ground. He was still conscious, but dazed, and attempted to get back to his feet.

Something gleamed in Lilac's hand. She moved at Emerson in a flash. He yelped in shock. His hands clutched at the knife wound. Blood welled from his stomach.

By the time Dan was back on his feet, rubbing the sore side of his face, Lilac was gone. He looked around in confusion, and spotted her moving silhouette a distance away, fleeing.

Emerson saw it as well. Still holding his injured stomach, he thundered after her with murder in his stride.

"I'll kill that bitch," he said through clenched teeth.

Dan stood as if in a daze before mustering the gumption to follow. He ran through the dark of night, down the grassy hill—toward the alligator pin, he realized a moment before he heard the scream. He froze.

At the brink of the alligator pin, Emerson had caught Lilac by her hair. She turned on him and struck several times in a blur, her knives slashing through his clothing and skin. Emerson retreated with a backward stumble and a startled exclamation, but not before Lilac seized the key ring on his belt.

She quickly found the lock on the gate. With a swift turn of the key, the lock sprang open and fell. The gate came open. Two of the alligators streaked out. Lilac ran aside as they went for the bleeding Alligator Man.

Powerful jaws crunched into the man's arm. He screamed and fought, only shredding his arm further in the alligator's teeth. In the fight, he lost track of the second one until it chomped into his head.

"You should feed them more often," Lilac said from where she stood, just outside the alligator pin with the bloody knife in her hand.

Dan could only stand with his mouth agape in the face of the horrifying spectacle. He shook himself to rattle his senses out of their shocked state. He ran.

"Help!" he screamed at the top of his lungs. *"She's killed Emerson!"*

Lights were lit inside several tents with a multitude of confused voices. People began to emerge. Among the first was an inebriated group of clowns.

Dan continued across the grounds, heading for Sutterfield's tent. The others heard his shouts clearly this time.

"The Alligator Man is dead?"

"She?"

Lilac walked up the hill and into sight. She held a long, bloody knife, one she had taken from Jackson's collection, and the one she had used against Emerson.

"It's her!"

The group of clowns confronted her. She brought a second knife into her other hand. With both blades held out at her sides she ran toward them. The clowns, some tipsy and some so drunk they could barely stand, stood no chance.

"Sutterfield!" Dan shouted once reaching the tent.

"What is it?" he growled. "What's the commotion? There'd better be a damned good reason for this." He stopped at Dan's pallor and terror-stricken eyes.

"Lilac," Dan gasped. "Emerson. He's—"

"I've heard enough!" Sutterfield roared. "I'll deal with this personally!" He stormed across the site, toward Emerson's tent. A pile of motionless clowns stopped him cold.

"Wait, Mr. Sutterfield!" Dan called after him. "Emerson, he's—he's dead!"

Sutterfield whirled around. *"What?"*

"She went in there!" a shout rang out. A group had assembled, acrobats and jugglers, and they pursued Lilac to another tent. They went in after her. Regaining a sudden hold on his wits, Sutterfield made a path for the tent in question.

Too late, Dan saw it was *his* tent. Realization seized him.

"No!" he screamed. *"No! Get away!"*

Pyrotechnic destruction blasted in all directions. The tent was gone in a nova of fire and smoke. A wave of heat accompanied the boom that threw Sutterfield to the ground.

"Mr. Sutterfield!" Dan ran to Sutterfield's assistance. Heavy footsteps from behind startled him. It was Jackson. Jackson shook Sutterfield, who coughed.

"Lilac," Dan whispered to Jackson.

"She did this?" Jackson looked in the direction of the blaze. Several other tents were on fire by now.

Smoke filled the air. Jackson held up an arm to shield his eyes. A thin form stood against the red blaze.

Jackson braced himself and strode toward the flames.

"Where are you going?" Dan called after him, incredulous, but he knew. Whoever, or whatever, Lilac was, whatever terrible force that had come to Sutterfield's Circus of the Fantastic, Jackson felt responsible. As such, Jackson meant to deal with it.

When Jackson drew closer, she hurled a burning ember at him.

Jackson threw himself to one side. Off balance, he wasn't prepared when Lilac ran for him. The blade sliced deep into his skin. His arm became slick with blood.

He thrust his own knife at her, which she spun to avoid. A knife in each hand, Lilac went for him again. Jackson ducked low and came up with a jab to her midsection.

His knife struck her. She didn't make a sound, almost as if she hadn't felt the pain. Instead, with a sudden blur, she drove both her own knives down into the soft areas between his neck and shoulder. His arms fell limp, and he collapsed.

Lilac stood over Jackson's body, the knives in her bloody hands, and stared toward Dan.

"Dan, what..." Sutterfield muttered from the ground.

"Mr. Sutterfield, get up!" Dan shouted. Sutterfield mumbled something unintelligible. Dan struggled to pull the large man to his feet. All the while, Lilac walked toward them.

Sutterfield finally came to his feet. Dan ran, and Sutterfield limped. Both of them fled to escape the wrath of Lilac. Behind them, the circus burned.

III

The phone's ring startled McCullough awake. He glanced at the clock. 3:53 a.m. He was supposed to begin to move to his new apartment in Wellville later today. Who would wake him up this early in the morning? He grabbed the phone from its receiver and knocked the bedside clock onto the floor in the process.

"Who is it?" he asked irritably.

"It's Sutterfield."

"John?" McCullough picked the digital clock up and righted it. "It's almost four in the morning!"

"A lot of good people died tonight."

"Died!" McCullough exclaimed. "What do you mean?"

"You're the only person I could think of," Sutterfield said. "I've seen a lot in my day, but I don't know what to say. This was a mass murder."

"Call the police. Call the police, John, and get yourself to safety."

"I'm safe. And I am calling the police. I'm calling you."

"I'm retired now. You know that. Call the police!"

At the other end of the line, Sutterfield went silent. He laid one hand on the double-barrel shotgun across his legs and leaned back in his purple cushioned chair. "I'm going to take care of this myself. Lilac won't get far."

McCullough only grew more bewildered. "Lilac? Look, John, don't do this. If you don't call the police, I'll call them."

"The police aren't fast enough." Sutterfield shoved shells into his shotgun. "Or dangerous enough. I'm settling this the old-fashioned way. Blood for blood. I just thought you ought to know. The circus was my life. Always was. Now it's all gone."

"Don't be stupid, John!" McCullough pleaded, but Sutterfield hung up the phone.

"Ready?" Sutterfield called. His eyes hardened when the response wasn't immediate.

"I—" Dan faltered. He cleared his throat. "I'm ready, Mr. Sutterfield." He loaded six bullets into the revolver, lent to him by Sutterfield, and tucked the gun into his pocket.

"Then let's go."

BLOOD FOR BLOOD

I

L	*ilac*. It wasn't a name McCullough heard every day, but it was familiar. Somewhere in the depths of his memory, a flare went off, something from his days on the force years ago.

While McCullough left his apartment and drove to-ward the circus grounds, Sutterfield's van moved past Candle Square and through the dark streets of downtown St. Charles. The van rounded a corner and sped up 3rd Avenue.

Sutterfield sat in the driver's seat, one hand on the wheel and the other on his shotgun. The remnants of his broken dream and career of over twenty years, Sutterfield's Circus of the Fantastic, littered his thoughts. Nervous, Danforth the Illusionist fidgeted in the passenger's seat.

Sutterfield squinted to look down each alley and braked at every passing shadow. She was out here somewhere, Lilac, a mere teenage girl who had single-handedly murdered several of his friends and circus per-formers. How she could ever have accomplished such an act, Sutterfield had no idea. He tried not to ponder it in detail. The fact was, it happened, and soon she would pay, as Sutterfield had told his old friend McCullough just minutes ago, blood for blood.

The shadow whisked along one side of the street. "That's her!" Sutterfield exclaimed. He pointed the shotgun out the window, took aim, and fired, but she was already gone. He turned the wheel and stomped the gas pedal.

The van accelerated down the alley after the fleeing figure. A garbage dumpster blocked the way ahead. He leaned out the window and fired again twice, but she dodged around the dumpster. The shells thunked into the rusted metal.

Sutterfield slammed on the brakes. The space around the dumpster was too narrow for the van to continue. He threw two more shells into the shotgun and jumped out of the van.

"I'll be damned if I'm losing her here," he said. "Come on!"

"But Mr. Sutterfield," stammered Dan. "I didn't even see anything!"

"She's here," Sutterfield said, and took off down the alley. Dan ran to keep up with him, dubious but thrusting a hand into his jacket pocket to grip the revolver. *Just in case.*

They moved down the alley. Sutterfield scanned the darkness and swung the shotgun barrel to the left and right. Movement sounded. Dan jumped, and Sutterfield aimed to fire, but saw a rat scurrying away through a garbage pile.

"Where are you?" Sutterfield demanded, his steps quickening. The search became frantic as he kicked over the overflowing garbage cans and aimed his shotgun into every dark corner.

"Mr. Sutterfield," Dan ventured, "I don't think she's down here."

"Of course she is!" barked Sutterfield. "I saw her! Don't be a damned fool! She's teasing us, waiting for us!" At that instant, headlights shone down the alley from behind them, in the direction of the van. Sutterfield shielded his eyes with one hand.

"John!" McCullough called.

"How did you find us?" Sutterfield asked.

"I knew you would be out here somewhere, and it just so happens that you're running around firing a shotgun at four in the morning, so it wasn't too difficult. I'm amazed you haven't gotten yourself arrested. What happened?"

"She ran down this alley and we followed her," Sutterfield said. He turned. "Do you hear me, you bitch? We know you're down here! Come out into the open!"

"Calm down, John," McCullough urged. "Are you sure she's even down here?"

"I know she is."

"Okay. Listen, we'll search the whole alley. If we don't find her, will you let the police handle this?"

Sutterfield didn't answer. McCullough joined them, and the three proceeded to scour the alleyway for any signs of Lilac. Other than a few more rats, the search turned up nothing.

"She isn't here," McCullough said.

Sutterfield's clenched jaw and infuriated eyes said more than enough. He remained unconvinced.

"Come on, John," McCullough said. "We searched the whole alley. She isn't here. She could be anywhere in the city by now."

Without a word, Sutterfield followed McCullough and Dan back up the alley to where the vehicles were parked. Sutterfield climbed back into the van, sullen, and set his shotgun down. Dan climbed into the passenger's side.

"We can talk about it tomorrow," McCullough said. "The police are going to be looking for her. They're at the circus grounds right now, and they'll need to talk to both of you about what happened. That's the best thing you can do right now. Okay?"

Sutterfield gave a somber nod. McCullough returned to his car and drove away. Sutterfield and Dan sat in the van in silence until Sutterfield released a heavy sigh of frustration.

"I'll find her," Sutterfield said, "and when I do, I'll blow her ass to kingdom come."

Dan shifted uneasily. "I'm sure you will, Mr. Sutterfield."

Just then, Dan heard the faint sound. He turned and he saw her. He grasped frantically for his pistol, but before he could gain a grip on it and before Sutterfield realized what was happening, she whispered into Dan's ear.

"I'm sorry."

The long blade penetrated the back of his seat and tore through him. He managed a gasp. Sutterfield shouted, fumbling with the shotgun.

The van's passenger side door opened. Lilac's figure darted around the back. Sutterfield fired through the back of the van. The rear window shattered. She fled down the street.

"Dan!" Sutterfield grabbed him by the shoulder and shook him. He coughed, and a froth of blood and spittle came from his lips. The life escaped his eyes.

Sutterfield leaped out of the van and ran after her. He pursued her through the streets, fired the remaining shell, and reloaded. She dodged into another alley, and he followed, firing again into the shadows.

"Freeze!"

Sutterfield whipped around at the sound. Two police officers held guns trained on him.

"Drop the weapon!"

"She killed him!" Sutterfield shouted at them. "And she's getting away! We have to stop her!"

"I won't tell you again! Drop the weapon or we will open fire!"

Sutterfield gritted his teeth, set the weapon down, and backed away with his hands in the air. The police officers rushed in and shoved him against the wall of the nearest building.

"You don't understand," Sutterfield fired as they handcuffed him. "You're letting a murderer get away!"

"No, *you* don't understand," one of the police officers said. "No one's getting away with anything. You're under arrest."

II

Sutterfield let out a weary sigh. The concrete wall pressed into his back, uncomfortable and harsh, but he'd be damned if he would lie down on that lice-ridden cot.

Dan was dead. The circus was no more. Sutterfield was behind bars, accused of murder. What the hell was happening?

"Mr. Sutterfield," called the officer. The bars slid open. Sutterfield stood to see McCullough standing outside.

"Took you long enough," Sutterfield said. The two walked out of the police station and to McCullough's car.

"Look, John," McCullough began. "It's pretty obvious to everyone that you weren't responsible. I told them what I knew, and they've checked out the scene. They're out there looking for her as we speak."

"She'd better hope they find her first," Sutterfield said. "Because if I do—"

"You aren't doing anything," McCullough interrupted. "You're going to let the police do their job. I'm really sorry about Dan. Really, really sorry. I know he was your friend. I'm also your friend. Listen to me. You'll get through this. Tonight, you need to rest and give the police a chance to catch up with her. I know some of those guys, John, and believe me, if anybody can do it, they can. Corbin and Pennington are on it also, and Corbin's one of the very best."

"What about the other guy?"

"He wouldn't be in the position he was if he wasn't also one of the best. Trust me. They're on it. Just give them time."

"I'll never rest while she's still out there," Sutterfield said. "And I want my shotgun back."

McCullough shook his head. "That isn't going to happen," he said. He opened the door to his vehicle. Once they were in the car, McCullough pulled out a brown sack. He removed a bottle from it.

"Finest bourbon there ever was. Tonight we'll kill this. We can talk about what happened whenever you're ready. Okay?"

Sutterfield didn't answer. McCullough sighed, threw the bottle into the back seat, and started the engine.

Newly sworn Detective Jacob Pennington, smoking a cigarette to one side of the building, watched them drive away. What McCullough was doing becoming in-volved with the situation, Pennington didn't know, but he did know he would have to watch his steps. After this onslaught, things were getting out of control.

Pennington had sold his badge long ago to the high-est bidders, the ones who were *really* pulling the strings in St. Charles. Tampering with evidence, misleading investigations, and following strange instructions which didn't seem to make much sense—though the tasks were far between, Pennington's position was uneasy.

How long would it be before they, whoever they were, had no use for him? How long before they released information about his involvement or before Corbin dis-covered the truth?

Pennington had come to fear the days when he would open his mailbox to find a manila envelope waiting inside. He tried once to install a surveillance camera in hopes of establishing the perpetrator's identity. One bullet to the mystery person's head, Pennington reasoned, would put an end to all of his problems. But what if *they* were more than one person?

It didn't matter. Somehow they had known about the camera, the way they knew everything else about him. The camera was destroyed, and he captured nothing on video.

There was no clear way out. Pennington finished his cigarette, stomped it out, and went back inside.

Now miles away, McCullough felt nagged by a memory that he couldn't quite place, a missing puzzle piece. He glanced at Sutterfield. "What was Lilac's last name?"

"I don't think she ever said."

"You don't check that sort of thing when you hire someone?"

"Wait," Sutterfield said. "I remember now, because of Dan. The two were getting close, or so I thought, until she killed him. Lilac Chambers. That's it."

The memories flooded back. McCullough's mouth fell open. *The Chambers cases, from years ago!* Those bizarre, unsolved cold cases that hung like a black cloud over his career for years, as well as Corbin's.

McCullough pressed down on the accelerator. Sutterfield glanced over at him, but remained quiet. Once they made it back, McCullough decided, he would call Corbin.

Somewhere in a dark alley, hidden and alone, a girl cried because she had killed the only friend she ever had.

1999

KILL

I

Retired Detective Brandt McCullough sat on the sofa of his apartment in Wellville. Wellville, the city of well people, where the peachy-keen retire to play golf. *Right.*

The phone was in his hand. He started to dial the number, and stopped, as he almost always did. He placed the phone on the sofa's armrest.

A voice on one end of his thoughts was full of reproach. *Why don't you call her?*

Because you tried calling her months ago, the voice on the other end of his thoughts admonished, *and we all know how terrific that went!*

Sandra had answered. McCullough had hung up. How long had it been now since he had spoken to his own daughter? If he called a thousand times, would he ever actually be able to speak to Nina? Not if Sandra had her way about it. It was the same story it always had been, wasn't it?

But what did he have to lose? Sandra had made plenty of threats, but what could she really do? Take him back to court? It wasn't as if he had seen or spoken to Nina in all these years anyway.

He snatched up the phone. He stood holding the phone, deliberating as he had many times before, when it suddenly rang. McCullough jumped, startled.

He answered it. "Who is it?"

"Brandt?" The voice sounded dulled by liquor, but McCullough would know that voice anywhere.

"John Sutterfield? Is that you?"

"Yeah, it's me."

"It's been a while. How the hell've you been?"

There was a lengthy silence. "I found her."

"Her?" McCullough paused. There could only be one *her* Sutterfield might be referring to. "Lilac Chambers?"

There was no reply.

"Have you called the police?"

"We let the police handle it back then," came Sutterfield's gravelly tone. "They never found her. And you know what? She's been out there for the past two years. The whole time, I've been watching, and I've finally tracked her down. I'm calling you because, with your help or without, I'm going after her, and this is going to end here."

"What? John, don't!"

There was a click. Whether McCullough liked it or not, he realized, the past had caught up with him again.

McCullough threw only what he deemed necessary into his travel bag and flung it into the trunk of his car. As a precaution, he loaded his .45 caliber pistol and brought it along. It was time to go back to St. Charles. Before he left, he made one final phone call.

Corbin didn't answer. McCullough left a message on the answering machine.

The drive was uneventful. The only break in its monotony was the occasional delay due to road construction. Eventually, almost two hours later, the familiar streets of St. Charles were beneath McCullough's tires. He made his way for Sutterfield's home.

McCullough arrived and walked across the over-grown lawn to the front door. The house's brown paint was flaking off, he noted absently, and then the barred windows caught his attention. Above the door, a security camera watched his every move.

He knocked and waited. After a minute, he heard Sutterfield's muffled voice from inside. "It's open." McCullough turned the doorknob and entered.

Sutterfield's home was a wreck. Dirty dishes were everywhere, and trash littered the floor. A cockroach skittered from beneath a week-old newspaper. Sutterfield reclined in his plush, but well-worn, chair. The chair's fabric was torn in several spots. A double-barrel shot-gun, remarkably identical to the one the police had con-fiscated from Sutterfield two years ago, rested in front of him on the scuffed coffee table.

While Sutterfield had been heavy before, he had since put on a considerable amount of additional weight. The coarse gray beard and shaggy hair indicated that he had gone without a haircut or shave in some time. The wrinkles around his eyes were far deeper than McCullough ever remembered. He wore one of his old outfits from the circus days, minus the top hat, and the old purple fabric had darkened from lack of washing.

Sutterfield held up a hand. "I know," he muttered, "I look like shit."

"Can't argue with you there," McCullough admitted. He looked around at the messy living room, and sudden-ly noticed just how hot and stuffy the place was. "Got an air conditioner in here?"

"A broken one. You're welcome to it."

"I can't believe you're living like this." McCullough kicked aside a heap of trash and fell into the neighboring chair. "If you'd even call it *living*."

Sutterfield shrugged. "Things change, don't they? I'm still around, though. I'm sure you noticed the cameras outside."

"I saw the one at the door."

"Not to mention the alarms I've had installed," Sutterfield said. He shifted in his seat. "They can't reach me here."

"They?"

"I've seen people sneaking around my house. You might think it's crazy, but I've seen them. The closer I've gotten to finding her, the more I've seen it happen."

"Are you sure you aren't being paranoid?"

"Believe me, my paranoia's kept me alive." Sutterfield grabbed a bottle of bourbon from beside his own seat and took a generous swig. He offered the bottle to McCullough.

"No thanks."

"Then let's get right to it," Sutterfield said. He corked the bottle and set it aside. "Like I told you on the phone, I know where she is. She's left a trail of murders for two years, but the police haven't been able to make any progress. People talk, though. Stories about her have spread throughout town. People know about her, but I'm thinking the only ones who actually see her end up dead. The police aren't even sure all of the murders are connected. Me, I'm sure. As sure as it gets. I've seen it with my own eyes, and I'm still here to talk about it." He paused, and decided on another drink. "I know her favorite places. No one can track her better than I can, and now I've found her."

"Because you've been obsessing over this for the past two years. If anybody knows where she is, it's you."

Sutterfield stood and shouldered his double-barrel shotgun. He walked toward the door. His path meandered with his drunkenness. He threw the door open. Dubious, McCullough watched him go.

"John –"

"Like I said, I'm doing this with you or without you." Sutterfield left the house. McCullough hesitated, but reluctantly followed.

II

He slid the needle into his skin and launched his obsession through his veins. He laid back on the futon, tossed the needle aside, and waited for the rush.

Whoever said money didn't buy happiness? It did for Quincy, at least for today. Without that crazy-large wad of cash, he would probably be dead in a gutter somewhere by now.

"Where's my money?" Johnny "Appleseed" Appleton and his boys would have demanded, the way they'd asked him the first time, right before they beat him to the ground and gave him a hard boot in the ribs.

The second time, though, that would've been it. Big Johnny Appleseed would have taken his baseball bat and broken every bone in Quincy's body.

But then the money came, and at exactly the right time, like the sort of divine intervention that Quincy always heard about but never experienced first-hand until today. Wasn't there some kind of saying about that?

Suddenly, Quincy just didn't care. The drugs worked their magic and he was on his way.

Hours later, Quincy Gershwin, a young man who knew too well the meaning of desperation, rose with a purpose: chasing the next rush. He almost tripped over his dirty laundry on his way out of the studio apartment.

He made his way down the aisles of the store. He selected everything he would need, hurried to the checkout counter, and threw it down. The clerk looked at him strangely.

"What?" Quincy asked. He looked around the store, anxious, and saw everyone staring at him. They weren't fixed stares, no, but they were watching him. Occasionally, someone would glance at him in passing, or the man in the nearby magazine section would look up from his motorcycle magazine to steal a look Quincy's way. They knew something was askew. Quincy wondered exactly how much they were able to tell just by looking at him. The man behind him murmured something.

"What did you just say to me?" Quincy asked the man, a hefty, bearded man in a flannel shirt with a case of sodas under one arm.

"Nothing," the man replied. Quincy thought about the sounds that came from the man's mouth a few seconds ago. He tried to piece them together.

"A waste of good oxygen if there ever was one," the man had said, or that's how it had sounded, now that Quincy thought about it. He looked back at the man again, but the man just stood there with his case of drinks, waiting behind Quincy in line.

"Sir," the clerk prompted Quincy.

"Just ring it up," he told the clerk.

"I already did," he said.

"Then what?" Quincy pushed.

"Thirty-two, sixty-six," the clerk repeated. Quincy pulled out the cash and handed it over. The clerk rang up the purchase and returned his change. Quincy grabbed the change, picked up his bag, and dashed out the door. The clerk watched his hasty exit without relish.

"What a nut job," the clerk muttered. "Next?" The line moved forward.

Once he was back at home, Quincy dropped his bag of purchases onto the floor and snatched up the letter. He scanned over it again and looked into his bag to make certain he had picked up everything. It was all there. Good.

One last time, he grabbed the unmarked manila envelope that had held the letter. *Don't worry about Johnny anymore,* the letter had said. Sure enough, Johnny Appleseed had turned up dead not long after. Whoever these people were, Quincy knew they didn't play around. If you were good with them, you were set. If you weren't, you were out of the picture. Quincy knew where he wanted to be.

He searched the envelope again, tearing it apart. The last of the money was gone. The time had come, then. More would come afterward. He threw the empty envelope in the floor.

He carried the shopping bag into the bathroom. After emptying the odd assortment onto the bathroom counter, he prepared himself and headed out.

Blocks away, Detective Pennington sat in his car, right down the street from the home with the peeling brown paint. He watched Sutterfield and McCullough depart. After a few seconds, he started the engine and trailed them at a distance.

Resting beside him in the seat was an empty manila envelope, much like the one Quincy Gershwin had earlier received. Beside the envelope were the latest instructions to accompany it. The piece of paper, small, plain, and white, was scrawled with three words: *Kill John Sutterfield.*

III

"I haven't been here in a long time," Becca said. "I can't believe you're making me come out here."

"What are you so afraid of?" Nick chided his sister. Becca looked around the park grounds. Summerset Park was dark and empty at this hour. The scent of lilacs was in the air.

"Satisfied?" Nick asked, after his sister had scanned the meticulously trimmed hedges that surrounded the park.

"Look, you know why I don't like this place," Becca said. "The same reason a lot of people don't."

"Because they're afraid *she'll* get them?" Nick laughed. He took a sudden step away from her.

"Come on out, Lilac!" Nick shouted. "Come and get us!"

"I'm leaving," Becca said, and turned to walk back the way they had come. Nick scoffed. He caught up with her.

"Look, why are you being so weird about it?" he asked. "And if you're so scared, why did you come out here in the first place?"

"I only came because you and Michael won't leave me alone about it," Becca shot. "But people really did die here. Two murders last year, and one this year. That isn't fiction. That's fact. People think it's her because of the stories, because of what happened at that circus two years ago. The reality is, it doesn't matter who it is. There've been murders in Summerset Park, and you're acting like an idiot about it."

Becca heard the soft footsteps a moment too late. The arm closed around her neck from behind. Her voice caught in her throat.

"Gotcha!" Michael shouted into Becca's ear. Her elbow plowed into his stomach, and he doubled over, gasping. Nick went into a fit of hysterical laughter.

"Don't you ever do that again!" Becca shouted at her brother's friend.

"You have to admit, he got you good!" Nick exclaimed, still laughing.

"Not as good as she got me," Michael said once he had caught his breath. He clutched his stomach.

"Come on, Becca," Nick said. "Chill. There's nothing out here to be scared of, okay?"

"I'm going home," she said. She walked across the park lawn.

"Get real!" Nick shouted. "You aren't pissed off over some little joke, are you?"

Becca neared the few trees that bordered the park's edge, and someone stepped out into her path. She stopped, a bit surprised, but her nervous edge was gone after Nick and Michael's prank. She was out of patience. She walked around the other girl.

"Watch where you're going," she said as she passed. At the last instant, she saw the knife.

Across the park, Nick and Michael heard Becca's scream. Nick started toward it, but Michael grabbed him by the shoulder.

"Hold up, man!" he said. "She's just screwing with us! Probably trying to get us back."

Nick hesitated. "Shouldn't we check just in case?"

"Are you really falling for that?" Michael pressed. "Seriously."

"Yeah, I guess you're probably right," Nick said. The two of them continued on, while far behind them, at the opposite end of the park, Becca's body sprawled on the grass and a predator slipped away.

IV

"She's not here," McCullough observed.

Sutterfield said nothing. He walked around the length of the old warehouse and kicked a few boards out of the way as he walked. With his shotgun in one hand, he moved some old sheets of plywood and peered inside a rusty oil drum.

"Empty. Damn it!" he kicked another couple of boards.

"What made you think she would be here?" McCullough asked.

"I had a lead," Sutterfield said. "From a reliable source, at that. Over the past couple of years, I've made the streets my eyes and ears."

"You might want to have your eyes and ears checked. There's nothing in here but rats and leftover lumber."

"We can wait it out until she shows up here."

"I'm not waiting all night in a place like this," McCullough replied.

"Suit yourself. I'm not going anywhere."

McCullough sighed dramatically. "I'm tired of playing this little game with you. You do whatever you want to do, but I'm not going to let you drag me through every little crazy scheme that pops into your head. Unless you can think of some other lead besides this, I'm going to get a hotel and catch a good night's sleep. Anything would beat staying out here." Instead of a sharp retort like McCullough expected, Sutterfield just nodded, appearing distant.

"All right," Sutterfield said.

"Good, let's get out of here," McCullough said, relieved.

"I really thought I had her this time." Sutterfield's tone was quiet, defeated.

As the two left, Pennington watched from his vehicle not far away, prepared to follow them again. His hands trembled on the steering wheel. He paused to mop the beads of sweat from his forehead.

The words still hit him like a battering ram. *Kill John Sutterfield.* Of all the tasks he had been given through the years, this was the first time they had instructed him to commit murder.

He took a deep, shuddering breath. His fear was getting the best of him. He had lived with his fear for years, along with all the doubts, and now it overwhelmed him.

"I can't do it," he murmured. "I can't do it. I just can't." He braced himself, and did what had felt impossible for so long. He defied them.

He turned down another street, desisting in his pursuit of Sutterfield and McCullough, and headed home. Somewhere well behind, another vehicle followed him.

Since Corbin had received McCullough's message, he had watched the perimeter of Sutterfield's home. Pennington's presence had been unexpected. He could have approached the other detective, but decided against it. Instead, Corbin decided to observe from his unseen vantage point. When Pennington followed McCullough and Sutterfield, Corbin followed Pennington.

The facts didn't add up. Corbin was determined to get to the bottom of it.

Corbin hung back while Pennington pulled into his driveway. Pennington reached over and grabbed the manila envelope from the passenger's seat. He walked to his front door and fumbled with his keys. When he slid the key into the lock, turned it, and entered his home, he didn't realize the door was already unlocked.

He shut the door behind him and moved to flick on the light. The needle pierced his arm before he reached it. His legs turned to jelly. The floor slammed into him.

"Home early, Mr. Pennington?"

Pennington felt groggy. It was difficult to move.

"It's…" He slurred the word. He tried again. "It's *Detective* Pennington."

"Oh?" His badge was plucked away. "You and I know that this means absolutely nothing, Mr. Pennington." The badge was tossed across the room, where it clanked into a corner.

Pennington forced his eyelids open. Two figures looked down at him, but he couldn't focus his vision clearly enough to make out their faces.

"Do you know who it is you truly work for?"

"No."

"And you never will. You failed to follow the instructions. It's a pity you could not have been more useful to us."

"No, wait," Pennington gasped. "Wait!"

"Nurse?" prompted the speaker. The other figure reached down, and Pennington could make out a syringe in her hand. The needle slid into the flesh of his neck. She depressed the syringe's plunger. The air bubble entered Pennington's bloodstream. His senses screamed.

Corbin sat outside for half an hour, watching Pennington's home. The house remained dark. Something didn't feel right.

He pulled his car up in front of the house and walked toward the front door with caution. Rather than knocking, he tried the doorknob and found it unlocked.

He pushed in and nearly tripped over his fellow officer's form. Pennington was dead on the floor. A manila envelope lay beside his body.

V

As Sutterfield stepped outside the warehouse, his cell phone rang. He fished it from his pocket.

"What?" he answered gruffly.

"I'm over by Summerset Park. There was a murder!"

Sutterfield stiffened. "What?" he repeated, attentive now. Hearing the dire note in his friend's voice, McCullough looked over.

"You told me to call if I saw anything," the voice on the phone said. "People just found a girl's dead body over here. The cops are on their way. Somebody said they saw someone running toward Candle Square."

Sutterfield rushed toward the vehicle with McCullough in tow. "Anything else?" he asked.

"That's about it," replied the voice. "But since I came through, I'll be wanting the fifty dollars you promised me." Sutterfield hung up.

"Candle Square," he said to McCullough.

They sped down the street. There weren't many out at this late hour, so McCullough was able to make haste toward their destination. They rounded the corner to one side of Candle Square. The outlets and businesses were closed, but the nightclubs were still open, given away by the music and neon lights streaming from them.

McCullough focused on circling Candle Square. Sutterfield scanned the area. The car passed a small group of late night bar hoppers and a younger couple walking hand-in-hand. After a distance further, they passed an old homeless man sleeping on the side of the street.

Coming from the direction of Summerset Park, a small-framed individual slinked through the darkness alongside a building. Sutterfield leaned out. He squinted to focus.

"Hold up," he whispered, and McCullough backed off the accelerator. The vehicle slowed to a coast. McCullough looked over, saw the object of Sutterfield's suspicion, and turned the wheel to make a near pass. When they drew close, both of them could make out the knife in her hand.

"It's *her*," Sutterfield breathed. He flung the passenger's side door open, right into her.

The door's impact slammed her backward. She stumbled, disoriented. McCullough punched the brake. Sutterfield jumped out with a shotgun leveled at her.

McCullough shouted at Sutterfield just before the shotgun went off. The weapon's explosion dropped her like a rock. Her blood ran across the sidewalk. McCullough stared in shock.

"Blood for blood," Sutterfield said. "That was the promise, wasn't it? And I finally got you, for everything you did."

The shotgun's blast roused a distant crowd to gather. Patrons from the nightclubs and other frightened bystanders stared toward the shadowed area where Sutterfield stood over the body.

McCullough shook his head, dazed by what his friend had just done. It was murder. One murder didn't justify another, did it? Or did it? Lilac had killed so many, but even intended as an act of greater good in this warped world, to take one life to save so many more— wasn't murdering a murderer still an act of murder?

His oldest friend had become a killer. As a man of the law, Brandt McCullough struggled with everything he stood for.

"We've got to get out of here," he managed, once he was able to grip a tangible course of action.

"Wait," Sutterfield said. His tone had changed. He crouched beside the body.

"People are coming," McCullough said from the car. "Get in!"

"It's not her."

"What?" McCullough asked. Had he heard Sutterfield correctly?

"It isn't her," Sutterfield repeated.

"Are you telling me," McCullough said, incredulous now, "that you just shot an innocent person?"

McCullough's fear and confusion gave way to anger. As Sutterfield stood, McCullough's fury overcame him. He leaped out of the vehicle.

Sutterfield turned as McCullough came at him. McCullough slammed a fist into his jaw and knocked Sutterfield against the nearby wall.

"You son of a bitch!" McCullough shouted at him. "You couldn't let it go, even after all these years! You couldn't just get on with your life. You had to wallow in your piss and misery, and look what's happened! You've dragged me down into your shit for the last time!" McCullough swung again. Sutterfield ducked. McCullough's knuckles met the wall.

Flesh cracked into brick with a meaty thud. Pain shot through McCullough's hand. He winced and fired a string of obscenities. His uninjured hand gripped the now bloody one. He turned toward Sutterfield again.

"You—"

"Brandt, listen!" Sutterfield said, in an effort to be the voice of reason for the first time since their reunion. "It isn't Lilac, but we didn't kill an innocent person."

"What are you talking about?" McCullough fired.

"The knife," Sutterfield said. He pointed at it. McCullough looked more closely.

"It's covered with blood," McCullough said, and puzzlement began to melt his anger.

"But it looks like Lilac," Sutterfield said. "The hair, anyway." He reached out to touch the long black hair, and looked up with a start.

"It's a wig," he said. "And something else. Not only is this *not* Lilac, but it's not even a female."

"What?" McCullough asked, stunned. Sutterfield went through the individual's pockets. Before McCullough could react, Sutterfield pulled a wallet from the body, flipped it open, and pulled out a driver's license. He held it up to his eyes.

"Quincy Gershwin," he read aloud. He stared hard at the face of the killer and back at the ID. "I don't believe it! The disguise, and the weapon. A copycat?"

"But the blood on the knife is fresh," McCullough stated. "He has to have been responsible for the Summerset Park murder. More than that, possibly, but it just doesn't—"

Police sirens became audible. They were still a healthy distance away, but filled McCullough with anxiety. The faraway crowd had grown to a substantial size now.

"We've got to get out of here," McCullough said. "We don't have much time."

"I just can't understand it," Sutterfield pondered aloud. "Is this the killer I've been tracking the whole time? What about the real Lilac?"

"We don't have time to discuss it, John. We have to go, right now."

Sutterfield responded with a nod. He gripped his shotgun and the two of them hurried to the car. An odd sense of discomfort gnawed at Sutterfield, prompting him to take a glance back. Lilac stood watching him— the real Lilac.

With a startled cry, he threw the shotgun from his shoulder. She came at him. He released a haphazard blast in her direction, but somehow, she was out of the way within a second.

On instinct, Sutterfield swung the barrel at her form. Lilac sidestepped, and it grazed her head. Though it hadn't caused any real damage, it gave Sutterfield just enough room to squeeze off the remaining shotgun shell.

Everything had happened so quickly that McCullough, on the other side of the car, had no time to prepare. After the first blast from Sutterfield's double-barrel shotgun struck the car, McCullough had his pistol in hand. Just before the second shot went off,

McCullough dashed around the car to get a better angle, unable to get a good shot off without endangering Sutterfield.

Sutterfield's second shotgun blast struck Lilac. Both she and Sutterfield froze where they stood. Lilac dropped to the ground a short distance from her mimic. The shot that downed her had struck her shoulder and midsection, McCullough could see. He turned to Sutterfield, and gasped at the sight.

Lilac's knife protruded from his chest. Sutterfield collapsed to his knees and fell onto his side. McCullough rushed over to him.

"I got her, Brandt," Sutterfield breathed. Blood bubbled from his lips. "For real this time." Lilac's blade had sank in handle-deep.

"Hang in there," McCullough told him. "The police are coming. We'll get you an ambulance. They'll get you patched up in the hospital before you know it."

McCullough wasn't sure if these words were meant to comfort his friend or to comfort himself. There was that insistent faraway voice, the one he refused to acknowledge, that told him John Sutterfield, his old friend, might not make it. Sutterfield's head rolled to one side. He coughed some blood onto the pavement.

"John," McCullough said. He shook his friend. No response. "John!" He grabbed Sutterfield by the shoulders and shook him again, roughly this time. That distant voice in his mind became more insistent. His eyes welled, and he shook his head. He struggled beneath the weight of the truth, until it crushed him, and the tears came.

The noise prompted him to turn his head. Lilac climbed to her feet.

A terrible hatred filled McCullough. He raised his pistol and fired. The bullet pierced her. She fell again.

He strode toward her, and saw her move on the ground, somehow still alive. He pointed the gun at her head.

"I'm afraid not. Not today."

The voice came from red lips plastered on a white face. It resembled a clown's face. Where had it come from?

"Nurse?" Clown-Face prompted.

McCullough felt the stick of a needle. He turned to see a woman dressed in a nurse's outfit, who had also seemed to appear out of nowhere. The drugs flooded McCullough's bloodstream, the gun slipped from his fingers, and he collapsed into a black sea of unconsciousness.

IN ITS SHADOW

I

McCullough woke in a dark, cramped confine-ment. He tried to sit up, but found this impos-sible. Weakness overtook him.

His memory began to return. The sense of motion entered his perception also, and probing the area around him with his hands, he realized he was inside the trunk of a vehicle. He reached into his pockets, and found they had been emptied. His gun was gone.

He thought about John Sutterfield, and sadness flooded him. When he thought about Lilac and the ones who had ambushed him, his sadness blistered into anger and became steel. This was not over, he knew, because for now, he was still alive.

The sense of motion halted. After a few more minutes of darkness, the trunk opened. McCullough looked into the barrel of his own pistol.

"Get out," the voice spoke to him. "Slowly."

McCullough climbed out of the trunk, an awkward process. He caught a glimpse of his captors, the man with the Clown-Face and the woman in the nurse's out-fit, a second before the gun's barrel crashed into his head.

McCullough smacked into the street. He heard a voice overhead.

"Stand up," it said, still quite calm.

McCullough stood, but felt the gun pressing against the back of his head. "Walk," came the command, and McCullough walked, guided by Clown-Face, the nurse, and the loaded gun to his head. They forced him through a darkened doorway and into what appeared to be some abandoned building. Down a short hallway, they entered a dark room with a single pale overhead light to illuminate an operating table.

Strapped to it was Lilac Chambers.

McCullough heard the flick of a light switch. The room came alight, bright white, and momentarily blinded him.

Lilac twisted around on the table. She moaned.

The gun remained at McCullough's head, and he remained motionless lest he suddenly have a skull full of lead, but his eyes wandered the white room, which had a certain sterile, *hospital* feel to it. In addition to the operating table, it featured a table in one corner that featured a variety of what appeared to be surgical tools, as well as needles and medicine bottles.

The clown-faced man, dressed in a white lab coat, came into McCullough's view. The face looked over McCullough's shoulder and spoke. "If he makes one small move," Clown-Face said, "put a bullet in his head."

The person behind McCullough, presumably the nurse, did not reply, but McCullough sensed she would not hesitate to comply. He remained still, with his hands at his sides, while Clown-Face stared at him with a hint of amusement in his painted face. The bright red lips opened to speak, but this was interrupted by a moan from the operating table. Lilac began to thrash against the restraints.

"Let me go," she hissed.

"I imagine you must be confused right now," Clown-Face said to McCullough. One side of the mouth twitched as if trying to keep a big smile from erupting across the face. "All will become clear to you soon. Very clear."

Lilac moaned loudly. Clown-Face looked to her, and he shuffled across the room to select a syringe from the table in the corner. Lilac raised her head with a snarl. Clown-Face approached to inject her, and Lilac's head thudded back onto the operating table. Her body stopped moving.

"This," Clown-Face said to McCullough, as he stood over Lilac's immobilized body and laid a hand on her forehead, "is only a vessel. Despite its human limitations, it has proven to be the most promising one." He stroked Lilac's hair. His head snapped up, and he went to the supply table to pick up a scalpel. He held it up in the light and examined it.

Despite the residual effects of the drugs and his dire situation, McCullough finally found words to speak. "Who are you?"

Clown-Face gazed at McCullough. "We," he said, "are servants. Servants of the Living Poison." He looked back down at Lilac.

"The human race continues to multiply," he said. "It continues to consume, expand, and destroy, and its toll will become an incredible burden on a planet of limited resources. It will see the future of an exhausted, destroyed world that is no longer fit to support the balance. But this end may be averted. A time of cleansing approaches. A time of cleansing, terrible perhaps through your eyes, but necessary if the world is to endure.

"Even as I speak, St. Charles stands in its shadow. The world will tremble before it heals. When the Living Poison has cured the earth of the human sickness, it will have been a privilege to serve the birth of this second chance for an otherwise ill-fated world. It is a privilege for my assistant and I, as well as for this one—Lilac."

The red lips curved in a smile. "We are the world's saviors."

The man was a lunatic, McCullough decided. "What is this Living Poison you keep speaking of?" he dared to ask.

"In less than one minute," Clown-Face said to McCullough, "I will show you. The Living Poison is only a poison in the metaphorical sense. You might liken it to a bacteria possessing a collective form of sentience, though ultimately this is also inaccurate, as the Living Poison is neither bacterial nor viral. It belongs to, and embodies, an entirely separate category. Observe."

To McCullough's astonishment, Clown-Face plunged the scalpel into Lilac's abdomen. The thin blade sliced cleanly through her flesh. She remained still.

He spread her skin open and peered down. His red lips parted and his eyes shone with reverence. He reached in and drew out a handful of bloody mush. The tissue was streaked with black, McCullough could see. Clown-Face looked up, and held the substance before him for McCullough to view.

"This is what makes *Lilac* what she is."

Clown-Face walked toward McCullough with the bloody clump of tissue in his hand. McCullough stared at it, revolted, until Clown-Face stopped in front of him.

"The way I see it," Clown-Face said to McCullough in a quieter tone, "you have two choices."

McCullough's heart thudded in his chest. He was afraid to ask, but knew the answer was coming. Clown-Face raised the handful of blackened, blood-dripping substance.

"You can join us," Clown-Face said, "or you can die. Those are your choices."

"Join you?" McCullough asked in a near-whisper.

Clown-Face held the bloody substance out to McCullough. "If you are willing to welcome the Living

Poison in, you will be allowed to live." Clown-Face observed the mixture of horror and confusion on McCullough's face, and added, "You must ingest this. Swallow it. That is the only way. Otherwise, my assistant will promptly put a bullet into your head. You have three seconds."

McCullough could only continue staring at it. "Two," Clown-Face said. Before McCullough could even gather another thought, Clown-Face said, "One." McCullough gathered every fiber of control he could possibly muster, and prepared himself for—he didn't know what. Could he do it? Could he swallow down that grotesque, blood-dripping mass? What would happen if he did? A sea of possibilities flooded his mind. He suspected the woman behind him was about to squeeze the trigger and end his life, and there was no possible recourse but to reach for that substance and try to force himself to carry through with that awful act.

A scream ripped through the air, Lilac's scream, and he faltered.

Clown-Face jerked, startled, and the gun wavered from McCullough's head for an instant.

It was now or never.

McCullough ducked, whirled, slammed a fist into the surprised gun-wielding nurse's stomach, and ran for his life, mentally preparing for the bullet that would smash through his skull as he fled.

The blast came. It struck the wood of the door frame. McCullough ran down the hallway beyond. The nurse stepped through the door to fire again. McCullough dove through the next door. The bullet flew wide of him as he struck the ground outside.

McCullough was on his feet in a hurry. He ran for cover.

Clown-Face and the nurse emerged from the building and looked around the darkened streets. The nurse searched for some glimpse of McCullough so that she might put a bullet between his eyes, but Clown-Face became anxious.

"There is no time," he said. "Others may have heard the shots. The moment is here."

Clown-Face walked back inside. After one last glance around, the nurse followed. They returned to the room where Lilac was restrained, and where that portion of her living tissue, that infested with the Living Poison, had fallen to the floor. Clown-Face retrieved it and held it up between the two of them.

They looked at it for several seconds in silence, and when their growing excitement could tolerate no further delay, they gulped it down with a frenzied glee.

Within the minute, Clown-Face and the nurse trembled. Clown-Face grabbed his head with both blood-covered hands.

Oh, how it has risen. What began as a mere seed from the Mourner's Cradle has become something so much greater than we could ever realize until this moment.

"I feel it," the nurse whispered. Clown-Face stood to make his way across the room, stumbling, and disappeared through the door. The nurse scrambled to her feet. She slipped in the blood, regained her balance, and dashed after Clown-Face.

"I feel it!" the nurse hissed again outside, louder this time. She and Clown-Face kept moving, through the next door and outside into the darkened night-time streets. They shook uncontrollably now. It rushed through them and overcame them.

"Our master!" Clown-Face shrieked. "We are one! We are one!"

They ran into the night, screaming until they encountered a random bystander, a man in a brown jacket.

The nurse whipped McCullough's pistol out and emptied every round into him.

The next victim was unprepared for the scalpel in Clown-Face's hand. It slashed across his face again and again. Teeth tore through his skin, bit into his shoulder and neck, and took flesh away.

An elderly man saw the grisly murder and shouted, but the nurse was on him, pounding his skull with the emptied gun. He crumpled beneath her savage blows. His cane skittered across the ground. Her shrieks rang through his dying mind. Her nails raked his skin and her teeth stripped flesh from his face.

She leaped to her feet, her hands and face covered with blood. The clown-faced killer, just across the street, flailed on another innocent pedestrian. By now, people were screaming. Their screams accompanied those of the two killers, who continued to dash through the streets and attack everyone in sight.

"God save us," a woman whispered. She fled until she spotted a pay phone. *Someone has to do something.* She dialed the police. The phone rang and rang.

"Please hurry," she urged in vain. After a few more seconds, someone answered.

"St. Charles Police Department."

"I'm at the corner of 7th and Berringer," she said frantically. "People are dying!"

They ripped her away from the phone and flung her to the ground. A final scream escaped her lips before they pummeled and butchered her in the street.

II

McCullough's first thought was to find help. He ran down the alleys and feared at any time that either Clown-Face or the nurse would pop around a corner and put a bullet into him, but this didn't happen, and not long after, he heard the screams.

He stopped and heaved to catch his breath. In the distance, he heard the gunshots. His eyes widened. Several shots. If it was his gun as he suspected it was, it was now empty. What was happening?

Call me crazy, his thoughts whirled, *but I'm going back to find out.* Maybe the drugs weren't completely out of his system yet, but this just might be the most idiotic thing he had ever done.

He looked around the alleyway and saw a pile of garbage, a board lying near it. On one end of the board, a few sharp nails jutted out.

He picked it up. It was better than nothing. He hefted it and took off toward the building he had so recently fled.

The gunshots had been much farther away, though, by the sound of it. Was it possible they had come from another gun?

He was already halfway back to the building. He would proceed with extreme caution. To do anything else might mean his death. He surveyed the door, and seeing no visible activity near it, he approached and gently opened it.

McCullough peered into the hallway. He saw no one. The pale light in the far room remained on. A scream froze him.

"Let me go," Lilac rasped.

McCullough started toward the door, holding the board at the ready, and looked into the room. He saw no one inside but Lilac, strapped to the table. One of the straps, he saw, had broken.

Lilac pushed against the restraints. Her ordeal had weakened her. McCullough wondered how long the straps would hold.

Lilac wailed with rage. Another of the restraints snapped.

McCullough stepped into the room. Lilac thrashed on the table, and an instant later, she stopped. McCullough halted where he stood. Lilac sat up and turned her head straight toward him.

The last of the restraints had snapped. Lilac's yellow eyes were cold. McCullough's heart pumped furiously.

She came down from the table, her midsection bare and bloody from the earlier incision. She spotted the nearby table full of surgical instruments, moved to it, and snatched a scalpel from its surface. She hurled it at McCullough. He moved back through the door. The scalpel clanged against a wall.

Within seconds, Lilac was in the hallway, a scalpel in each hand. She leaped at him. He swung the board. It struck her across the face. The nails raked flesh away. Lilac landed on him, knocking him to the ground, and she stabbed wildly with both scalpels.

He struggled to deflect her blows. He dropped the board in the process. Her attacks were erratic. Everything became a blur of insanity. McCullough felt a scalpel slash his shoulder, another strike in his midsection, and another sliced across his cheek. He cursed, gained a hold on the board again, and rammed it into her stomach. He jabbed it upward and it struck her in the face. She fell backward. A scalpel clattered to the floor.

Lilac came up again, the remaining scalpel in her hand. She came forward in what McCullough first thought was a lunge in his direction, but she stumbled, and McCullough realized that she was weakened.

Lilac seemed to realize this as well. McCullough saw it in her eyes, the longing for his death, but there was something else—trepidation. Instead of attacking, she scrambled right past McCullough and ran for the door.

McCullough held fast onto the board, and used it to help himself to his feet. He nearly slipped in his own, or Lilac's, bloody mess on the floor. For extra protection, he grabbed the nearby scalpel dropped by her and tucked it into a pocket.

He turned and ran out the door after her. He thought about his friend John Sutterfield and the countless other lives taken by Lilac, and there was no doubt in McCullough's mind that, if he allowed her to escape, she would kill again.

III

The streets were in chaos. The killing spree had blazed down 7th Street, leaving several dead bodies in its wake before the police arrived. The men in blue, together with Detective Corbin and Chief Watkins, swarmed out. They formed a wall of defense against the bloody clown-faced man in the lab coat.

"Freeze!" Watkins yelled. He trained his weapon on the individual, who stood over a fresh victim even now.

Clown-Face walked toward them.

"Last warning," Watkins called. "Stop now or we will open fire!"

Clown-Face bolted toward him. Watkins squeezed the trigger. A flurry of bullets cut down the clown-faced killer. The white lab coat went red.

An officer looked to the chief, and Watkins nodded. The two of them edged forward.

"Fan out," Watkins called back to the others. "We need to assess exactly how much of a crisis we've got here."

Corbin looked around at the carnage, at the bodies in the street. His mind raced. What had happened here? And why? He hadn't seen anything like this since…

Since that massacre at the circus, years ago. He remembered it, Sutterfield's Circus of the Fantastic, and he remembered something else.

John Sutterfield had been found dead. So had Detective Pennington, whose demise had led to the discovery of his corruption. So many fragile lives lost, just like that.

The figure on the ground moved. Clown-Face writhed, pressed both hands against the ground, and began to rise.

"Stop!" Chief Watkins shouted. He aimed his weapon.

A figure flew out of nowhere and bashed a police officer to the ground. Dressed in a blood-covered nurse's uniform, it was hardly recognizable as a human female. She swung and tore at him in a frenzy. He struggled for his life.

Corbin, nearest, moved in and fired. The side of the nurse's head exploded onto the street.

Her victim shuddered. The nurse's blank eyes stared down at the officer from a partially revealed skull. He heaved to push her body aside, but he was too weak. Corbin was quick to come to his aid, and shoved the body off him.

The officer's breath came in labored gasps. His throat was a mess of mangled bloody tissue. The other officers rushed in. While Corbin and the rest tended to the downed officer, from the corner of his eye, Chief Watkins saw the motion.

Clown-Face stood. He moved toward Watkins, his movement slow and exaggerated, reminiscent of a puppet.

"Don't move!" Watkins shouted. His words went unheeded.

He fired. Several bullets tore through Clown-Face, and he dropped to the ground again, for the second and last time.

Chief Watkins looked back to the fallen officer, where Corbin and the rest were gathered. Corbin met the chief's gaze and shook his head.

IV

McCullough ran through the street, scalpel in his pocket and board in his hand. Lilac was quick, and though weakened, she had a head start.

The Living Poison, a diabolical force to destroy humankind, to poison and eradicate. He couldn't allow Lilac to escape.

She might kill me, but I'll make sure I'm her last victim, because I'll drag her down with me.

"Lilac!" he shouted. He could still see her moving form well ahead, shrouded by the dark of night. She showed no signs of slowing. He pushed himself harder in pursuit.

McCullough mentally cursed himself. Why hadn't he alerted the police when he'd had the chance?

What's done is done. If he had not come back, Lilac might have escaped to take another life. Now, wherever the chips fell from here, it was just Brandt McCullough and Lilac Chambers.

Adrenaline and fierce determination pushed McCullough through the alleyways, around corners and across the street after Lilac Chambers. Memories of her terrible crimes, and the wrecked life of his old friend John Sutterfield, fueled him.

Lilac, and the Living Poison inside her, had destroyed lives in a swath of suffering and death. If she escaped, there would be more to follow.

They raced up the street, toward the River Bridge. He pursued her across the bridge, over the river far below. To McCullough, everything around was a blur of dark fog except Lilac's fleeing form, until she stopped to face him. McCullough, heaving for breath, advanced.

Her yellow eyes studied McCullough. She held up her scalpel, prepared to slice him to ribbons.

McCullough had driven across the River Bridge more times than he could ever count. He never imagined he might spend the last seconds of his life here in a scalpel fight with such a creature.

It all hit him at once: his place in the lives of everyone he knew, and his role in his daughter's life, a daughter who didn't know him, and who might never know him.

The past was full of wasted opportunities. The only sliver of hope that remained was in the future. Whether or not he would be here to see that future, he didn't know. He gripped the board and moved forward.

"Goodbye," Lilac said, and turned to leap over the edge of the bridge.

McCullough ran for her, but he was too late. She cleared the bridge. McCullough, knowing no alternative, leaped through the air after her.

He swung the board, a useless motion. There was too much distance between them for it to connect. The river rushed up to meet them. A wall of water slammed into them from beneath, wrenching the board from McCullough's hand.

Dazed, McCullough plunged through cold, dark waters. He fought to hang on to consciousness and to hold his breath. The river's undercurrent threatened to pull him down. He raged for the surface with every ounce of his strength.

A hand grabbed his ankle. The sharp pain came next, unbelievable pain, as Lilac's blade sliced into his tendon.

He almost gasped, but fought against the pain and shock with every fiber of control he could grasp, and only the mental image of his own lungs filling with frigid water saved him from losing it.

He kicked at her with his other leg. The underwater resistance slowed his movement, but he kicked several times until she released his ankle. He swam upward as best as he could. The pain in his ankle was excruciating.

He shoved a hand into the pocket that contained the scalpel. In the underwater dark, he couldn't see much of anything, but was now aware of something behind him. He spun around in an awkward motion. Her blade grazed his side. He wasted no time in stabbing at her with his own scalpel, and the blade punctured solid flesh.

He stabbed again and again. She slashed at him. Her scalpel raked his cheek. The dark water went darker yet, clouding with blood. McCullough fought for his life. He stabbed Lilac several times, jabbed at her face once he became aware of her position in front of him, and drove his scalpel through the flesh of her throat.

She flailed, and McCullough struggled to pull away. Her form went slack. As she drifted, the undercurrent seized her. Suddenly, she was gone. His lungs about to burst, McCullough pressed his wounded, strained body toward the surface of the river.

Deep in the river, the life drained from Lilac Chambers. She felt it inside, the Living Poison, its terrible hunger now devouring the only life that remained for it—her own.

Lilac's mouth opened, and water flooded in. She flew on the wings of freedom from life itself. The current dragged her body down and the forces of nature washed it into limbo.

McCullough broke the surface. The night sky met his vision. He could do little but gulp in the fresh air until his spinning thoughts began to stabilize. He made way for the bank.

After crawling up onto the muddy ground, he scanned the river's surface for several minutes. The river flowed on, its waters quiet and certain. McCullough laid back on the ground and stared up at the stars.

She's dead. I should be, too.

"But I'm not," he answered himself aloud. He pulled himself into a sitting position and winced. He eyed his bleeding ankle.

"Mister?" came a voice. He looked over his shoulder. An old man approached. "Are you okay?"

"Yeah," McCullough replied. The man came closer and saw McCullough's ankle. Wide-eyed, he looked over the numerous other cuts and wounds covering McCullough's body, including his face.

The old man spoke again, saying something about people falling off the bridge and asking about an ambulance, but McCullough couldn't remember exactly. Next he knew, he found himself among the cool, clean white sheets of a hospital bed. His wounds were bandaged, and he was attached to an IV. Or the IV was attached to him. However that worked. Though weak and loopy from the pain medicine trickling into him, he reminded himself that he was still alive.

He came close to jumping out of his skin when he saw the nurse, despite the pain relief, but calmed himself within seconds. Nurses spooked him now, it seemed, and from now on, he imagined clowns would as well.

"Corbin," he told her. "Detective C. J. Corbin of the St. Charles Police." The nurse gave him an odd look, but left the room. An unknown amount of time later, McCullough was gratified to see Corbin standing near his bed.

"What on earth happened?" Corbin asked him. "I heard they found you out by the river."

"It's over. After all these years, and all the deaths."

Corbin didn't speak right away. He seemed puzzled.

"Lilac," McCullough clarified. "Lilac Chambers. The Living Poison. No one else has to die because of it."

"What are you talking about? We got the killers, and the body of the Summerset Park Killer was found near Candle Square. The stories about Lilac aren't true. That's a myth."

"No, it's true," McCullough insisted. "Search the river if you don't believe me. Her body's there."

"But that doesn't work for me either, because—"

"It's true!" McCullough shouted. Corbin stepped back, surprised by the outburst. McCullough lowered his tone, but the edge remained. "It's true, Corbin. Search the river, and you'll see!"

DOWN IN THE VALLEY

The St. Charles Police Department worked with diligence to comb the river. The people of the valley watched and gossiped among themselves. Stories of the massacre of 7th Street from a week ago accompanied incomplete accounts from some who claimed to have witnessed an incident near the bridge. A particular hysteria hung over the region, but that was the least of the police chief's concerns.

"Chief!" an officer called. "We've found something. You'll want to have a look at this."

Across the town of St. Charles, Brandt McCullough finished unpacking. *At least that part's finished,* he told himself. Moving the last time hadn't really felt worth it, after all was said and done, but this time was different.

True, there were bad memories in St. Charles, as well as some good ones. This was his home, and he had lot of both. He drew back the curtains and gazed out the window.

Returning to the couch, he took the bottle from the coffee table, uncorked it, poured a drink, and let it swirl in the glass before holding it up.

"For you, old friend," he said to the memory of John Sutterfield, friend and lifelong man of the circus. He downed the bourbon.

He clinked the glass down on his coffee table, maybe not so much a coffee table as a bourbon table. After another moment, he poured himself another drink. As he raised it to his lips, the phone rang.

"Hello?" he answered.

"This is Corbin."

"Good to hear from you," McCullough said. "How's everything?"

"We found a body in the river. Since you're the one who gave me the tip, and also a friend, and we went through a lot during our time on the force, I thought you should know."

McCullough sat up. He took another drink of bourbon, and drained it most of the way this time.

"The thing is," Corbin continued, "for all you told me about Lilac, this doesn't make a lot of sense."

"What?"

"The body we found is a skeleton."

McCullough nearly spilled what was left of his drink. *A skeleton?*

It had only been a week ago. The body wouldn't have decomposed to that extent already. Would it? *No.* The cogs in McCullough's mind spun.

"You still there?"

"I'm here."

"Like I said, I just thought you should know. The more we proceed with this investigation, the more loose ends seem to be turning up. I'm also going to need you to come down to the station and answer some more questions. Can you come today?"

"Give me around an hour," McCullough replied.

That was the end of the call. It would later be confirmed, through extensive research, that the skeleton was indeed that of Lilac Chambers. The dental records matched. McCullough would take solace in this, but there would remain that lingering doubt he couldn't ignore.

Servants of the Living Poison, they had called themselves, blinded by devotion to a force so chaotic that it led them willingly to their deaths. Words remained in McCullough's memory.

A day of cleansing. The world will tremble. He looked over his shoulder often, with the fear that, irrational though it seemed, the Living Poison might still be out there in some form.

Today, he just finished his bourbon. The unease permeated his thoughts already, although he hadn't yet identified it.

Another thought came to him, one that had visited countless times in the past, and especially of late. With a fair amount of bourbon in him, he picked up the phone and dialed the number.

"Hello?" came the answer.

"Nina?"

"This is Sandra." A pause. "Is this Brandt?"

"Look, Sandra," he said, "I don't want to fight with you. I don't want anything in the world from you. I'm tired. I just want to talk to my daughter. That's all I ever wanted."

There was another pause, a longer one this time. "She doesn't live here anymore."

"What?"

"She moved out sometime ago and got her own place. But do you want my personal opinion?"

"Not really," he said, and hung up. He flipped open the phone book, and was gratified to find the desired entry. *Nina McCullough.* Beside it, a phone number. He dialed the number.

"Hello."

Her voice was so different. The last time he had ever heard it, she was a small girl. He struggled with the words. What could he say to her after all this time?

"Who is this?" Nina asked.

"It's—" McCullough shook his head, and began again. "It's me."

"Who's *me?*"

"It's your father." He waited for the click, but it didn't come.

"I've been trying for so many years," he added. More silence followed.

"I'm so glad you called me," Nina finally said.

"You're *glad?*"

"I've wondered." Her voice was quiet, and sincere. "Through the years, even though mom told me that you wanted no part of my life. And then one day, out of no-where, I got a phone call. He said he was a friend of yours. He told me about you. He told me that you had always wanted to be a part of my life, and that had al-ways loved me, despite anything. I didn't know what to think. After that, I really started to wonder."

McCullough could swear that he'd heard tears be-hind her voice. *That makes two of us.*

"A friend of mine?" McCullough asked. "Did he say what his name was?"

"John, I think. John Sutterfield. Is that it?"

"Yeah. That's it."

McCullough went on to speak to his daughter through the following hours, which would cause him to be very late for his meeting with Corbin and the St. Charles Police.

Meanwhile, down in the valley, on the river bank, the fishermen were back at work, hauling in the day's catch. The stories about the skeleton found in the river continued to circulate, but there were families to feed and lives to be lived. The fish were biting like crazy to-day.

"I haven't seen anything like this in a long time!" exclaimed one of the old fishermen. Some of the others nodded their agreement. No one complained. At the end of the day, a celebration was in order.

The smell of sizzling fish wafted through the air. The people of the valley gathered in abundance for the fish fry, and everyone ate heartily.

"Haven't seen anything like it in a long time," the old fisherman repeated to himself, his belly full and his thoughts swirling in a strange fashion.

His mind wandered back to the activities of the day and all the fish he had caught. Something had been out of the ordinary, something about their attitude, even though they were just fish. *Piranhas,* he thought. That's what they had reminded him of with the way they fought like crazy.

It was sort of like the strange feeling inside him now. He felt it growing, the poisonous transformation taking root in his core, and so did everyone around who had consumed the tainted fish. Down in the valley, almost everyone felt it.

ABOUT THE AUTHOR

Tommy B. Smith is a writer of dark fiction, author of *The Mourner's Cradle* and the short story collection *Pieces of Chaos* as well as works appearing in numerous magazines and anthologies through the years. His presence currently infests Fort Smith, Arkansas, where he resides with his wife and cats.

More information can be found on his website at http://tommybsmith.net.